DATE DUE          MAY 05

| 726 | | | |
|---|---|---|---|
| | | | |
| | | | |
| | | | |
| | | | |
| | | | |
| | | | |
| | | | |
| | | | |
| | | | |
| | | | |
| | | | |
| | | | |
| | | | |
| | | | |
| | | | |
| | | | |
| | | | |
| | | | |
| GAYLORD | | | PRINTED IN U.S.A. |

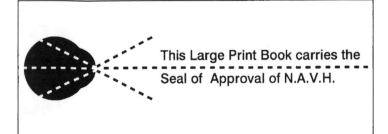

This Large Print Book carries the
Seal of Approval of N.A.V.H.

# KALEIDOSCOPE

## Yesteryear

# KALEIDOSCOPE

## Book Two:
# Yesteryear

## Perspective Changes in a Suspense-Filled Romance

# Gloria Brandt

**Thorndike Press • Waterville, Maine**

*Yesteryear* Copyright © 2001 by Gloria Brandt

Scripture quotations marked KJV are taken from the King James
Version of the Bible.
All Scripture quotations, unless otherwise indicated, are taken
from the *Holy Bible, New International Version*®. NIV®.
Copyright © 1973, 1978, 1984 by International Bible Society.
Used by permission of Zondervan Publishing House. All rights
reserved.

Published in 2005 by arrangement with
Barbour Publishing, Inc.

Thorndike Press® Large Print Christian Romance.

The tree indicium is a trademark of Thorndike Press.

The text of this Large Print edition is unabridged.
Other aspects of the book may vary from the original edition.

Set in 16 pt. Plantin by Al Chase.

Printed in the United States on permanent paper.

---

**Library of Congress Cataloging-in-Publication Data**

Brandt, Gloria
    Kaleidoscope : yesteryear : perspective changes in a
suspense-filled romance / by Gloria Brandt.
      p. cm.
    "Book two."
    ISBN 0-7862-7387-9 (lg. print : hc : alk. paper)
    1. Secrecy — Fiction.   2. Large type books.   3. Romantic
suspense fiction.  I. Title: Yesteryear.  II. Title.
PS3602.R363K35 2005
813′.′54—dc22                         2004028080

---

To Dad and Mom . . .
for being patient
with all my scribblings then —
and supportive of them now.
Thank you.

As the Founder/CEO of NAVH, the only national health agency solely devoted to those who, although not totally blind, have an eye disease which could lead to serious visual impairment, I am pleased to recognize Thorndike Press* as one of the leading publishers in the large print field.

Founded in 1954 in San Francisco to prepare large print textbooks for partially seeing children, NAVH became the pioneer and standard setting agency in the preparation of large type.

Today, those publishers who meet our standards carry the prestigious "Seal of Approval" indicating high quality large print. We are delighted that Thorndike Press is one of the publishers whose titles meet these standards. We are also pleased to recognize the significant contribution Thorndike Press is making in this important and growing field.

Lorraine H. Marchi, L.H.D.
Founder/CEO
NAVH

* Thorndike Press encompasses the following imprints: Thorndike, Wheeler, Walker and Large Print Press.

# Prologue

*15 August 1853*

---

The woods are beautiful. Deep. Lonely. Isolated.

The last plank of floor was laid today. My sense of "lost" is only overshadowed when encompassed by the newness and excitement of the pending school year. The odor of fresh wood is such a heady aroma. It smells of . . . future. Truly, each step through my new classroom fills me with anticipation . . . and more than a fraction of doubt. Thoughts of my father's warning flutter through my mind. . . . "Is one of such a tender age capable of this task?" But my resolution returns — with each dazzling sunset, with each songbird's trill.

No, in spite of the vastness of this new land, I am convinced that the Almighty placed me here for a purpose. It is that thought that keeps me from shivering in complete cowardice when the noisy coyotes howl in their nighttime ritual.

How shall I ever bear the following weeks? How shall I ever endure the solitude? My resolve set aside, I cannot help but wonder . . . is the molding and teaching of young minds to be my only life's calling? Or is there more?

Thank you so kindly, Mr. Longfellow, for leaving that ponderous gap. . . .

"No one is so accurst by fate,
    No one so utterly desolate,
But some heart, though unknown,
    Responds unto his own."

I pray it might be so. . . .
                        — Madeline Whitcomb

# Chapter 1

The fly buzzed noisily through the stifling air in the cramped office. Jack Tate swung at it impatiently with the brown felt hat still clutched in his hands.

"Are you sure you won't reconsider?" Bob Feldman leaned across the small, cluttered desk, inadvertently shifting a pile of papers askew.

Jack shook his head without hesitation.

Bob tilted back in the creaking chair that seemed entirely too small for his ample frame. His graying brows rose a fraction . . . then he nodded. "All right. I still think you might be selling yourself short, though."

A dubious stare was all Jack returned, followed by a lopsided grin.

"Okay, okay," Bob chuckled. "Have it your way. What do I know? I only run the place." He twisted around to look at the quickly filling calendar on the wall. "When's the first group scheduled to arrive?"

Jack squinted at the dates. "I . . . uh . . . next Monday."

The older man scribbled something undecipherable on a pad in front of him. "Good enough. And everything's set for supplies?"

A nod.

"You've checked in with Paul? He has all the blacksmithing materials he needs?"

"Mm hm."

"Looks like you've done your job well . . . as usual." He offered Jack a smile of encouragement. "Just wish — well, that you could be more involved."

Jack promptly placed the dusty hat back on his head. "This . . . is fine." With a departing smile, he yanked open the door that always determined to stick and stepped into the hot, early June sunshine — an intense load off of his mind.

She picked dejectedly at the fraying threads hanging from the knee of her tattered jeans. How long had they been out there anyway? She flopped backwards on her bed, wishing she could just go to sleep. But even that seemed to elude her lately.

From outside her closed bedroom door, she heard the voices. Talking quietly, hushed. Afraid she might hear. No matter. She already knew what they were saying anyway. The same thing they'd been saying for the last few weeks. Since the funeral —

No. She would not go there. *Think of something else, anything.* . . .

Soft footsteps approached down the hall.

She quickly assumed a more natural sleeping position on her small bed and took a deep breath before the knock came.

"Carillon?"

*Mom.*

She didn't move.

"Honey?" The door creaked open, and the sliver of light from the hall barged its way into her self-made dungeon of darkness.

"Lon?" Dad that time.

She released a silent sigh. If they were both here, there was no getting around it. Stretching, she rolled over and squinted at them in mock sleepiness.

Approaching with a cautious air, her parents stood next to the bed. Her mother finally settled lightly on the edge, the concern in her blue eyes evident. Carillon looked away. She didn't want to see it. She didn't deserve it.

"Lon," her dad started, "Pastor Jim is here. He'd like to see you if —"

She shook her head adamantly. "No, I don't want to talk to your holy roller pastor!"

This time the sigh belonged to her father.

She took the sign of disapproval as the cue to roll back over.

From behind her, she felt her mother's hand brush gently across her arm. Carillon didn't pull away as she might have several months ago, but the contact didn't strike any chord within her, either. She was empty. Always would be. She was an awful human being — no, a monster.

"Honey," Mom started, "we're worried about you. It's not . . . natural to stay in here like this. Cloistered."

She remained motionless. Silent.

"Rachel," her father said quietly, "let me."

She felt her mother slowly move off the bed, only to be replaced by her father's slightly larger and heavier form.

"Lon." He cleared his throat somewhat nervously. "We've been talking to Pastor Jim. We think we've found something, or rather someplace, that might help you."

For the first time in a long, long while, Carillon felt something. The quick surge of panic rushed through her veins as her clouded mind raced with a host of unthinkable outcomes of this conversation. They'd stick her in a mental institution or some hospital. Or maybe jail. After all, it had been her fault that —

"Lon, do you hear me?"

She tried not to shiver.

"Turn around, please."

For once, she didn't have the courage to brush the request aside. There was an earnestness in his voice she'd not heard — not lately. She gingerly maneuvered herself over. But she still couldn't meet his eyes.

"This isn't healthy," he began. "And your holing up in here isn't helping you, us, or anyone else."

"So . . . what?" she replied edgily. "You want me to throw a party? Have all my friends whom you love so much over here?"

"That's not what we meant."

"Of course, it isn't. Nothing I do would be right anyway."

He seemed to ignore her last comment and forged on. "We think you need to get away for awhile."

Here it came. What hospital would it be? And how long would it take her to break out of it?

He laid a pamphlet down on her comforter. "We've gone ahead and made the arrangements for your arrival. You can pack tonight. The bus leaves tomorrow morning."

Bus? Tomorrow? Every part of her being wanted to jolt upright and scream, "What!"

But she did nothing. Said nothing. It was routine now — trouble caught up with her, consequences around the corner. Until she found her way out.

But this time . . . This time it was different. She might just deserve it. Or at least need to rid her parents of her lifetime of mistakes that tarnished their lily-white name.

Apparently her parents were waiting for some sort of reaction from her. Why, she didn't know. They ought to know by now. . . .

Her father fingered the pamphlet one last time, then tentatively reached over to stroke her hair. But he stopped a few inches from her head.

Keeping her gaze glued to the cotton comforter, Carillon watched his arm fall in resignation before the two of them left the room in silence, pulling the door shut behind them. She collapsed back onto the bed, letting the now-welcome darkness envelop her once more. She heard the slip of paper slide to the floor. She hadn't the energy to retrieve it, much less flick on a lamp to see what it might say.

No, all she wanted right now was the darkness. So no one could see her. Even herself.

The long walk back to Jack's "quarters" was quiet, pleasant. It gave him a chance to be pensive without the occasional distractions of work — and visitors. Only the varied chorus of birds provided the background for his welcome solitude.

Underneath the lacy canopy of giant evergreens and maples, he trudged along the well-worn path, finding his destination purely by instinct. He could have walked this in the pitch black of night — indeed, he had. More than a few times. Recently . . . and long ago. An involuntary shiver skittered down his back.

Sloughing off the latter portion of that thought, he came to the clearing that marked his home. Stopping, he assessed it with a critical eye, trying to see it as one would for the first time.

The small, sturdy log cabin sat peaceably beside a stand of pine trees. Behind the white chinked structure stood the weatherworn barn; a chicken coop, complete with cackling guineas; and the building least liked by any employee of Yesteryear . . . the outhouse. He smiled, remembering the arguments that seemed to ensue every year among the staff: Couldn't they just put hidden "modern" bathrooms in the various locales?

Resuming his study, he wondered . . . was everything in place? Anything missing? All miscellaneous, unnecessary items properly put away? It just wouldn't work to have a visitor stumble across a stash of old Pepsi cans while traipsing around the one-hundred-year-old barn's manger.

Removing his hat and once more assessing his plain brown trousers and light-colored work shirt, he nodded to himself. From here on out it was the fifties.

The 1850s.

Nighttime had finally come. For real. Carillon could pull up the shades in her room and let the natural blackness invade the space. Time seemed irrelevant anymore. She couldn't measure hours, days, weeks. Even months and years were fast congealing into an abyss of bad memories and guilt. She found it preferable not to dwell on it at all. The continual hum of the digital clock and the rustling of her bedclothes were the only sounds she knew now. On occasion when she had to go into her small, adjoining bathroom, she ignored the light switch. She wanted no reminder of herself appearing in the bathroom mirror. The ghostly hush was broken only by the

16

sound of splashing water.

Tonight there were a few stars. Faint little pinpricks of brightness in the vast expanse above. For some unknown reason, Carillon reached out and pushed open the window — just this once. Just to let a little bit of the cool night air blow on her face.

It nipped at her cheeks ever so slightly, its dampness settling around her.

She closed her eyes and inhaled deeply.

At least tonight there was no moon. Nothing to illuminate the reminders of her own stupidity, carelessness, selfishness . . .

No wind. No movement to bring even the sounds to her —

*"Carillon . . ."*

Her lids flew open. Her heart stalled for a split second.

Silence.

She stood from the window seat and stumbled backwards.

*"Carillon . . ."*

Around the enormous lump in her throat, she managed a breath. "Evie?" she whispered.

No response.

A different, new courage overtook her. She lunged at the window and flung it open wider. "Evie?" she called desperately into the evening breeze.

Down the street, a lone dog barked out a warning. All else was still.

But she'd heard her. She knew she had.

Plucking her pillow from the bed, she propped it up against one end of the window seat and settled in. If Carillon heard her again — she'd be ready.

# Chapter 2

The bus jostled and swayed along the curved, tree-lined road. Carillon knew that out the rear window the last telltale remainders of the city had slipped away . . . somewhere between the suburbs and the increasing rolling hills. If she'd a mind to, she could have turned around and watched as all she knew stayed behind on some paved street while the rest of her was whisked away. Each bone-rattling bounce from the gravel path's potholes made it more than apparent. She'd never been one to lament much of anything. That would have entailed giving a rip about something, and she didn't. Not anymore.

It was clear why her parents hadn't told her of their plans until last night. With such short notice, there was no opportunity for her to run away — hide. Finally she was at the mercy of their "do good" ideals. She didn't want it. She didn't need it.

Facing a span of hours with nothing else to do, Carillon finally relented and pulled out the pamphlet from her duffel. *Yester-*

*year. A place of history and healing.*

She frowned. *A place of . . . what?*

The little paper was overloaded with Bible verses and photos of ancient-looking buildings. In and around them were people of all ages, apparently dressed to match the surroundings. This was where she was going? And what did they expect her to accomplish there?

She read on and discovered it was a tourist-type place. Apparently the "workers" were people such as herself. And during the summer months, people came to visit the living history museum — to see life as it might have been lived more than one hundred years ago.

Carillon's frown deepened. She was going to have to be Laura Ingalls for the summer?

*No,* she reminded herself — *only for a little while.*

Shoving the leaflet back into the pocket of her duffel, she tried to doze as the eternal stretch of hours, which might as well have been days, finally ended and the aging vehicle ground to a stop. With the roar of the engine now quieted, the slow patter of the persistent drizzle made itself known against the dusty windows. She knew some of the others aboard, probably filled with equal amounts of curiosity and dread, were

20

straining to see through the watery streaks what would be their "home" for the next three and a half months.

Three and a half months . . .

She still couldn't believe her parents had pawned her off for that long. No matter. It just gave her more time to plan and execute her escape. Then she wouldn't have to trouble her family or anyone else ever again.

In spite of her resolve not to care, she couldn't keep her eyes from straying upward and outward, just for that initial glance.

Before she could take in much at all, a fresh-faced, college-aged girl covered in a bright orange slicker stepped up into the bus. "Good afternoon!" she said cheerily. "Welcome to Yesteryear. If you'll all just grab your bags and things and follow me, I'll take you into the main meeting hall, where we'll go through the orientation material. There are snacks and beverages there as well, so come on in and relax."

Carillon studied the girl. She looked young, in a carefree sort of way. Like she hadn't a care in the world. And why would she? She obviously wasn't there for any reason close to Carillon's. What did these people know about real life when they were stuck out here in the middle of la-la land?

For the first time, Carillon looked around her at the hodgepodge group trailing off the bus. She wondered why they were here.

Waiting until the last passenger had disembarked, she flung her khaki duffel over her shoulder and stepped down the aisle and out into the light rain that covered everything in a gray mist.

Her eyes settled on Yesteryear. Amid the drizzle, four log buildings of varied sizes were situated in a rectangular shape, the one long, open end of a neatly mowed courtyard facing the parking lot where she now stood. Behind all of the white chinked structures stood a continuous row of huge, towering pines.

Out of all the overgrown cabins, the only two clearly labeled were a restaurant and a gift shop. The other two, she guessed, were the non-tourist buildings. Most likely where she'd be staying.

None of them looked genuinely old, but they'd obviously been built to seem that way. Rustic, to say the least. And not exactly what she'd had in mind for her summer months, even before Evie had —

Squeezing her eyes shut and shaking her head adamantly, she bid the thoughts away . . . for the moment. It was only a matter of time until they came back.

For now she had another job to do. Another person to become . . . just until it was all done.

Jack wrapped the slicker closer about his neck as he peered up from under the brim of his hat. Cold rain. The crops were never going to grow if they didn't get any decent warm weather for more than one day at a time. The rain-slicked grass on the path had already turned his boots a moist dark brown . . . and most likely his socks as well. He'd have to remember to put more oil on the boots when he got back home later.

As he neared the building compound that housed the offices, gift shop, restaurant, and sleeping quarters for some of the staff, he heard the roar of the bus driving away, the spittle of gravel being showered back upon the road.

So, they'd made it. The first group was here.

For some reason he'd not yet been able to define, that same sense of apprehension, nervousness, and disquiet nagged at him. The same as the last five years. He'd tried to sort it out. He'd prayed about it. He knew why he was here and that he believed in what Yesteryear was doing. But it still came. Maybe not so much apprehension — more discontent. Thus far he'd been able to brush it aside as he immersed himself in the ever-present duties that needed his overseeing. It was enough — for now. Later . . . ? He'd trained himself not to worry about later. What would come would come. One day at a time.

As he rounded the last stand of giant pines that lined the compound's perimeter, he saw a lone figure standing in the middle of the self-made courtyard among all the buildings. Minus any sort of coat or hat, her long dark hair hung limply down her back, clinging to the equally soaked shirt she wore with a rather tight mini-skirt. She faced the other direction, not seeming to be looking at anything in particular.

She was small, slight. And for a brief moment Jack wondered just how young they were taking these people anymore. But he also knew that physical build could be deceptive. In spite of his own twenty-five years — and at least a dozen of those being spent at muscle-building farm labor — he'd more than once been mistaken for a teen himself. It had bothered him at first, but he'd gotten over it. Wasn't much he could do about it anyway.

As he approached the building, he de-bated about whether or not to issue an invitation in — and quickly thought better of it. But maybe if she saw him going in, he could at least hold the door open or offer some nonverbal suggestion for entrance.

Making a point of walking rather noisily past her quiet spot, he was halfway to the wooden steps of the restaurant when her smooth voice stopped him.

"Do you have a cigarette?"

He halted in his tracks. Then slowly turned around. The look on her chiseled face was fairly unreadable. No hint of a smile tweaked the wide, full lips.

"N–no . . . smoking allowed," he stammered, suddenly embarrassed.

A quiet, albeit troubled, smile lifted her high cheekbones. Jack quickly realized he'd been an idiot to have thought her a child. Looking at her face-to-face more than told him this was no kid. Pretty obvious. In a lot of ways.

"I know," she said simply.

He looked at her quizzically.

"The no-smoking rule," she clarified. "I knew." She gave a small shrug. "Just tryin' to break the ice."

The rush of warmth flew up his neck and into his face. This girl was getting the best of him and he'd not even met her yet. With a resigned chuckle, he threw a glance at the ground before remeeting those knowing eyes. He noticed her twitch with an involuntary shiver.

Berating himself for being dense, he whipped off his slicker and tentatively held it out to her.

She blinked at it, almost in confusion, before raising her wet lashes and staring at him. Jack saw that familiar flicker of distrust . . . then something else. A brief softening? Too quickly it vanished. And with an equally hesitant hand, she grasped the proffered article and shrugged into it, looking uncomfortable. "Thanks," she said softly.

Turning around, he motioned with his head for her to follow as he started toward the stairs once again. At the door, he held open the heavy wood portal and waited for her to enter. She paused at the threshold and eyed him more carefully. That same disconcerting scrutiny that made his ears burn. He shifted his gaze to the sign just above her head on the door.

"You're shy." The mirth in her voice, obvious.

He returned her direct look and tilted his head in possible acquiescence.

"Do you have a name, Mr. Shy Gentleman?"

"Hey, Jack!" the voice carried across the

restaurant's foyer with ear-ringing clarity. He swung his head in the direction of Paul, the blacksmith, and gave him an informal salute. "Bob's waiting for you in the office. Something about the bulk food order."

With a nod, he closed the door carefully behind the young woman whose name he did not yet know. He wished he could ask.

She held out a slender hand and shook his warmly. "Nice to meet you, Jack. Think I'll go and change clothes." She unwrapped herself from the abundant leather slicker and started to hand it back to him.

He shook his head and took a deep breath. "You . . . k–keep it." With a quick glance out the window, he indicated the continuing rain.

Her lips drew into a private smile. "Thanks again." Without another word, she moved gracefully across the empty dining room toward the far hall. And Jack tried to remember the last time his pulse had pounded that loudly in his brain.

"Here's the list." Bob handed over the clipboard with a pen. "Not as large a group this time. Should be easier to assign without so much doubling up."

Jack nodded as his eyes roved down the paper. Of the twenty-some names before him, more than half were female. He wondered which one belonged to her.

". . . And the last of the animals were supposed to be delivered this morning."

Lifting his eyes from the sheet, Jack realized he'd just missed half of what had been said. "Really?" He tried to wing it from there.

"They took 'em over to the usual barn at the Hanson place."

"G–good. I'll run over . . . and check on them . . . r–right away."

Bob looked up from his disorganized desk for a moment, concern on his round face. "You okay, Jack?"

He made a point of restudying the names in front of him and let out a breath. "Sure. W–why?"

The older man lifted his shoulders. "Your . . . speech seems a little more choppy today. Everything all right?"

Embarrassment mingled with gratitude as the man's concern made his face flame — again. How many times was that today? With a self-deprecating chuckle, Jack tilted his head. "F–first day . . . I guess. I–I . . . gonna be . . . okay."

Bob gave him an understanding grin and a hearty slap on the shoulder. "Alrighty then. We'll see you tomorrow morning. I'll be anxious to see what you work out for those interpreter positions. Everybody's file with age and experience is in there."

Jack tapped the sheet. "Tomorrow."

"Hi, I'm Lydia. What's your name?" the slightly plump girl with incredibly thick glasses asked cheerily.

Carillon sighed and shifted her attention from the trees outside the window back into the crowded room where they were all seated, waiting to get their first overview of Yesteryear and some preliminary instructions. "Carillon. Carillon DeVries."

"What an interesting name. However did you get it?"

She threw her a placating look. "My parents were poor spellers."

Her antisocial answer must have sufficed. The curly black head nodded in a moment of confusion before turning to the person on her opposite side — with much better results probably.

Yeah, well, friends she didn't need. Not here. All she needed to do was get ahold of Leslie. If they ever got this ridiculous meeting over and done with. She glanced at the clock one more time.

With her chatty neighbor's attention shifted elsewhere, Carillon made it a point to peruse the room. She hadn't seen him

29

again. This . . . Jack guy. Not since she'd first come in. Cute enough — even if he was a little on the scrawny side. But more than that, he'd made her initial job easy. By the look in his eyes and his quiet manner, he seemed like the soft type who was more than willing to . . . "help."

But from somewhere inside, she felt an uncomfortable pang. There was something else about the guy. . . . Something that reminded her of someone else. That softness, that openness — wanting to trust.

The look could have been Evie all over again.

Evie.

The pounding in her head returned, and she pushed her fingers against her temples. *Oh no. Not now. Not here.* She was away from that now. This was where it was supposed to end —

"Okay," the businesslike voice echoed from the front.

Thankfully it broke the game her mind was trying to play.

"Welcome to Yesteryear. For those of you who aren't familiar with our facility, I'll give you a brief introduction. This land, all seven hundred acres of it, was purchased by a private party in 1992. Since that time, careful selection of numerous historical sites, buildings, and farms has been made. And each, in turn, has been disassembled, moved here, and carefully reconstructed as a permanent part of Yesteryear.

"We do a fantastic tourist business in the summer months, and the inclusion of people, such as yourselves, helps us out in the summer season when we especially need the extra staffing.

"There is, however, a bigger reason for Yesteryear's existence. Due to the philanthropy of a caring, Christian man, this place has become something of a haven for those who need a healing touch. You're all from different circumstances and backgrounds. But we're all here to work together, support one another, and ultimately let God touch us in a way that happens only when we totally surrender ourselves to Him.

"We hope you find that surrender while you're here — and that Jesus Christ will meet you in a very profound and lasting way."

Carillon began to squirm under the religion this guy was spouting. She should have known the place would be some "churchy" thing . . . the idea coming from her parents' new pastor. Ever since they'd gotten involved in that bizarre place several years ago, she'd seen them take on some pretty peculiar habits. Bibles lying all over the house. Different music coming out of the CD player. She'd even caught each of them, at various times, on their knees, praying. Sometimes right in the middle of the living room. Just weird.

But what made it worse was that they'd gotten Evie mixed up in it. She was just a kid. How was she supposed to defend herself against that at her young age?

"Today's session," the man continued, "will entail our ground rules, including conduct, etc. Tomorrow there will be a tour of the whole facility — every farm and house and store that's a part of what we call Yesteryear. From there, your job assignments will be given out. You might all expect to be 'tour guides,' or what we call 'interpreters,' but that may or may not be the case. There are positions as wait staff in the restaurant, checkers in the gift shop, and so on.

"So, if you'll all turn to the second page in your booklet we handed out, I'll point out the first items we'll need to discuss before . . ."

His voice droned into monotony as Carillon listened with half-open ears. Listening only for anything that might give her more information. Anything inside. All the while, keeping her eye out for Mr. Shy Jack — her possible ticket out of here.

# Chapter 3

"I was told we got to make phone calls." Whether or not Carillon had a grip on her current, raging frustration and anger, she didn't know. Nor did she care. All she knew was that this perky little college grad in front of her was messing up her plans in a major way.

"I'm sorry. . . ." The young woman glanced quickly at Carillon's name tag. "Miss DeVries, phone privileges aren't extended until everyone's finished the week-long orientation. If there's some sort of emergency, of course, we'd be happy to —"

With a scathing glare, Carillon cut her off. "Fantastic. I'll see what I can do to come up with an emergency. Thanks . . ." She looked just as pointedly at the small badge on the employee's chest. "Miss Zahn. You've been a big help." Stalking away, she ripped her own identification tag from her T-shirt and tossed it into the nearest trash can. These people didn't have any clue what they were dealing with here. How hard could it be to escape from the middle of nowhere? No bars. No walls. No one standing guard.

But she needed to get hold of Leslie. Somehow. Fast.

The narrow hall that lined the perimeter of the restaurant angled off into a deeper corridor. A quick glance around told her no one seemed to be in the vicinity. The majority of the group had stayed in the main conference room during the break, chatting. She had better things to do.

Taking a determined step down the hall, she listened carefully for voices. She heard an occasional muffled conversation behind the several closed doors she passed on either side. At the turn of a corner, the hall ended abruptly with one door leading outside. The small window framed the dismal day and the offices of Yesteryear that lay fifty feet or so across the compound. On her immediate left, a door stood ajar several inches. Peering around the entrance, she noted a room flanked with shelves holding a variety of food stuffs. In the center was a small desk. With a phone.

Carillon bit her lower lip in concentration and slipped into the empty office, quietly closing the door behind her. Stealing over to the corner of the desk, she cautiously picked up the receiver and listened for the dial tone. With one more glance at the door, she punched in a rapid sequence of numbers, chewing on her thumbnail while each ring intensified her paranoia.

Someone picked up and fumbled briefly with the phone. "Hello?" a groggy female voice mumbled.

Carillon frowned. "Leslie?" she whispered.

"Hello?" the young woman said, following it with a yawn. "Who's this?"

The pulse points near Carillon's temples began pounding in aggravating rhythm. She felt her senses tightening along with her grip on the receiver. "It's Carillon," she returned caustically, then cringed, remembering to keep her voice down.

"Lon?" Leslie's voice sounded surprised.

Great! She'd been gone how many hours now? And her best friend had already forgotten?

"Where are you?" Leslie mumbled. It was pretty obvious her brain was in no mode for thinking.

"You know where I am!"

"Oh . . . yeah."

Carillon's grip on the phone tightened, her nails digging into the palm of her hand. She suddenly wished desperately that it was Leslie's neck in her grasp. "Have you and

Kari got ahold of a car yet?"

"Oh . . . no. I guess not."

"Les!" She bit her lips together, inwardly reminding herself to hush up. "Forget it," she breathed in exasperation as she slid her hand through her hair. Yet again, she'd have to rely on herself. As usual.

"Lon, hold up!"

Carillon slammed the phone down and took several deep breaths while the dull thud in her head intensified into a piercing ache.

Outside the door, distant footsteps echoed down the narrow hall. Her breath catching in her throat, Carillon slipped to the door and gently latched it, engaging the small lock. Then she turned and made a quick assessment of her surroundings.

Behind her, a hand tried the door knob.

Skittering behind a stack of flour bags, she crouched between the huge sacks and the wall, just as a set of keys jingled from outside and one found its way into the lock. She hoped whoever it was didn't need any flour.

With her back against the wood-planked wall, her chest heaving in silent breaths, she waited. There was shuffling through some papers on the desk. And a clipboard suddenly plunked on the stack of flour, right near her head. Unable to completely stifle the quick intake of breath, Carillon held it deep in her lungs. Clenching her eyes shut, she waited. . . .

Some minutes later, after some canned goods had been removed from one of the shelves, the person plucked up the clip-board and, from the sounds of it, exited the office and closed the door.

Hardly daring to release a breath, she peered over the wall of white bags and waited again. Just in case.

Confident she'd let enough time elapse, she slid out from her hiding place and padded toward the door. With a careful hand, she twisted the knob and peered around the jamb. Empty. Leaving the door ajar, as she'd found it, she walked briskly down the hall and stepped back into the common hallway that led back toward the conference room.

"Do you need help finding something?" A man's authoritative voice stopped her short.

"Just looking for the rest rooms," she answered after a moment's hesitation. She glanced over to find a large, round-faced man holding a slew of papers.

"They're the other way." He indicated with his free hand. "Opposite side of the restaurant."

"Thanks." She gave him a half smile and continued on her way.

She'd made it.

And now, apparently, the rest of it was up to her as well. Why she thought she could ever rely on Leslie or Kari for anything . . . She cut off her own thoughts, not ready to bring to the surface those betrayed feelings again. She could do this on her own. Like before. Only one thing she needed . . . just a little more information on the layout of this place. And she knew exactly where to get that.

Jack sat at the rough wood table, bent over the collection of papers before him. The kerosene lamp's flickering flame cast dancing shadows over the vellum sheets. With a heavy sigh, he grabbed the large mug and took one last swig of the cooled coffee. Outside, a particularly brisk shot of wind slammed against the log cabin, making the front door shudder on its broad hinges.

Shoving the file away, he leaned back in the wooden chair, balancing on its rear legs. Done. Everybody had a job to do. Barring any unforeseen personality or ability conflicts, the assignments should work out well. Having a chance to see each person's background drastically increased his insight as to which jobs should be given where.

But for the first time in his five years working at Yesteryear, he'd found his line of concentration broken more often than not. Riffling through all of the women's portfolios first, he tried in vain to discover who the girl he'd seen earlier might be. He wondered why it should matter anyway. He'd learned a long time ago that girls like that were meant for a definite type of guy. And he definitely wasn't it. *Like it's of any consequence,* he railed inwardly. *Do your job, Jack. Remember, you and she are here for completely different reasons.*

But her expressive eyes refused to leave his memory. And he found himself searching for clues again. He really didn't have any idea as to her age — and the records covered everyone from fifteen to forty-four. Even the names were no help, really.

Although, one name had stuck out . . . simply because he'd not heard the word in so long — Carillon.

He'd done a double take at that, then had chuckled. One of his mother's favorite words. "Listen," she'd say as the summer dusk settled around their farmhouse porch. "They're ringing the carillons." To Alice Tate, an incurable romantic, the carillons were the steeple bells from the small country church several miles over the rolling farmland. They announced the twelve and six o'clock hours more faithfully than any practical clock radio.

As a child, Jack had wondered just who had the incredible task of getting to the church well ahead of time and climbing up those narrow tower steps to ring that monstrous bell. Something straight out of *The Hunchback of Notre Dame.*

His own fanciful notions, surely fueled by his mother's own love of literature, had been dashed when his older brother, Jon, had laughingly explained they were on a timer. No one rang them by hand. Not anymore. Jack found that thought sad. He always thought that ringing those bells would be an awesome thing.

But as always, Jon would bring him back to earth, reminding him that anyone with his build would have an impossible time even keeping a grip on the thick rope. Jack had bristled at his brawnier brother's assessment but knew it most likely was true. Still, he spent many a night out in the garage, trying to lift the weights that his brother so effortlessly used to sculpt his thick arms and chest. He knew he got stronger . . . but not much bigger.

But back to the name — Carillon. Carillon. Her exquisite beauty could be worthy of such a title, but he'd also learned long ago not to get too wrapped up in the thoughts of the imaginary. They didn't get one too far . . . especially men, it seemed. Unless one really craved ridicule and scorn.

With a long breath, he eased up from his chair and took the lantern with him toward the sleeping quarters in the loft. One goofy name was sending him back on all sorts of past roads in his memory — ones he didn't need to travel down again. Once had been more than enough. From there, he'd given them over to God, almost imagining the "Road Closed" signs his heavenly Father had erected. No, there was no reason to dwell on things that he couldn't change. Even if he was left with painful reminders —

Shaking his head in annoyance, he deftly stepped up the homemade log ladder and set the lantern near his thick pallet on the beam floor. The loft was high, adding nearly another story to the one-room cabin, so standing near the peak was no problem. He hung his clothes on the nearby pegs, crossed over to the stash of food and smoked meats that hung on one end, and took down a slab of bacon for his morning breakfast. Placing the meat near the ladder, he settled himself down next to his Bible, once again grateful for the privacy his loft bedroom afforded. Most of the other interpreters had theirs on the main floor of their residences, but considering the number of tourists who traipsed through the cabin, day in and day out, he desired slightly more privacy. For his rest. For his things.

For his memories.

He opened the yellow, worn pages of the well-used Bible and leaned on one elbow as he reclined. "Ok–kay, Lord," he murmured with a half-smile. "W–what do You have . . . for me . . . today?"

# Chapter 4

Jack stared out at the group before him, trying not to let his knees quake in total cowardice. The last eternity had really only been approximately eight and a half minutes. Approximately. It might as well have been a year. Trying to simultaneously look official and at ease (something he wasn't sure was working), he shuffled the papers in front of him and glanced at the clock once more. Bob had said he'd be back before nine. It was almost ten after now. The small gathering was getting louder as they passed the time, talking among themselves.

Jack threw one more look back at Steve at the rear of the room. His friend shrugged and gave him a "go for it" nod.

Jack cleared his throat.

"G–g–good . . . morning." That got their attention. But it was pretty obvious for the wrong reasons.

He shifted his weight and frowned at the papers in his hands. "I'm here . . . t–to as–s–s–ign you t–t–to your jobs." He blew out a long breath and tried to ignore some of the curious faces staring straight at him. *Help me, Father. Make this ridiculous tongue work.*

"John . . . Wilson." That was better. He just needed to slow down. "You'll b–b–be working . . . with P–p–p—" He stopped and took another subtle breath. "With . . . Paul. The black . . . smith." One down. Twenty-three more to go. His brain went dizzy.

At that moment, Bob sauntered into the room, looking harried, red-faced, and winded. "Sorry," he panted as his large form moved to the front. "I got a call at the last minute." He reached Jack's side and indicated the sheets before him. "You wanna finish up?"

Jack shook his head and gratefully handed the stack to his boss, trying not to run to the nearest chair before collapsing into it.

Bob took over with the professionalism he'd gained over the years. His booming voice resonated through the room, and there were no whispers, no chitchat, only rapt attention. Jack sat in amazement — only wishing he could command such a presence.

He sat slightly slumped over, his arms leaning across his knees, trying to get his heart rate back down. It was racing not just from his attempt to speak to the crowd, but in anticipation. Somewhere down in the middle of that list was the name Carillon DeVries. And he was dying to know if it was her. And if not, who exactly she was.

But much to his disappointment, the name and assignment came and went with no indication of the person's identity. No, he'd just have to make his rounds of the place and see where she might be. He still had an inkling that name belonged to her, so he'd try the gift shop first. That's where he'd assigned Carillon — whoever she was.

When Bob had finished going through the list, he dismissed the group to head to their new locations to start training immediately. Jack stood and tried to nonchalantly look in that girl's direction. She was near the back, sitting with a couple of the other younger members of the group — ones who looked to be less than thrilled to be here. There were always those in the group. Not all came voluntarily.

When he saw them making small talk, he casually started for the back of the room. Maybe he'd overhear her name in the conversation. A couple of times, he even saw her smile. It was a beautiful smile . . . if somewhat subdued.

Shouldering his way past a small clump of employees, he managed to slip through the door just behind the young women. With their attention ahead of them, he could follow undetected. Instead he concentrated on what their voices were saying.

"I'm in the restaurant," one girl mentioned, seeming apathetic to the placement.

"I got stuck at some farmhouse," another complained.

Then she spoke. "I guess mine isn't too bad. Clerking in the gift shop."

His heart lifted a fraction. He'd been right. It was her.

"Or," she continued with a light laugh, "should I say 'the g–g–g–gift sh–sh–shop.' "

Her two companions laughed with her as they streamed through the front door out onto the grassy compound.

Jack sank against a nearby wall and frowned, trying to swallow the hardness in his throat. Why the comment should matter, he didn't know. He was used to it. But for some reason, the words hurt a little more today.

Jack spent the remainder of the morning and a good part of the afternoon doing the animal chores at his own farmstead. It normally didn't take that long, but it was a way to kill his day. There was a lot to be done, what with the tourists beginning to arrive in less than a week. But even he couldn't fool himself out of the real reason for throwing himself into the consuming tasks. Each pitchfork full of straw, each wheelbarrow full of grain, each swing of the hammer on the split rail fence did nothing to relieve the ache in his mind — and his heart.

He was so stupid.

He'd done it again.

He'd let himself get caught up in a foolish notion . . . a dumb dream. Just like Jon always said he did. It seemed like one burning disappointment was enough to teach him a lesson for awhile. But sooner or later, his heart would run away with itself again. Letting him think he was things he was not. Things he would never be. Places he would never go. Dreams he would never accomplish.

It must have been awhile since the last time, because that one stupid comment from that unknown young woman was sending him reeling farther than he had in quite some time.

*Well, buck up, Jack. You asked for it. Letting a silly name grab you and running with it. You're still the same. Always will be.*

He sank one last spike into the fence, trying to release some of the pent up frustration. He knew he'd need some extra time

47

with the Lord that night. It was the only soothing balm that ever eased the hurts — even the physical ones.

He shook his head. *Don't even go there. You don't need that on top of everything else.*

He strode toward the small barn, hammer in hand, when he saw a familiar form emerging from the trees. It was Steve. And he looked concerned.

Tossing the tool in the doorway, Jack met him halfway across the lawn with a friendly smile. "Hi. Everything . . . all . . . right?"

Steve shook his head. "It's the usual, Bud. It's just happened a little sooner than normal."

Jack nodded in understanding. Every year, without fail, there were one or two new people who invariably caused problems during their stay at Yesteryear — usually at the onset of the summer. But it ordinarily took a few days, at least.

"S–s–so who's . . . the t–troublemaker . . . this t–time?"

Steve pulled out a file and handed it to him. "A Carillon DeVries."

Jack swallowed a little hard.

"She's at the gift shop. Apparently her performance today has already proven to Ruth that she'd be less than 'ideal' in the customer relations department."

Jack glanced at the file and kneaded his temple.

"Ruth is already talking to her about it. Seeing if that would help."

He nodded as he continued to flip through the pages.

"But," Steve added, "I got the distinct impression she'd be more than a little relieved if you assigned our guest elsewhere."

Jack nodded again and released a long breath. "Okay. I–I–I'll see . . . what I–I can do."

Steve gave him a sympathetic smile and patted him on the shoulder. "Better your job than mine." He grinned and threw a wave over his shoulder as he disappeared into the thick stand of pines.

Striding toward the house, Jack tossed the papers on the table and paused at the washbasin to rinse off some of the afternoon's dust and sweat from his face and neck. He poured a glass of water from the nearby pitcher and finally realized how hungry he was. He'd worked straight through the day, not stopping for breakfast or lunch. And judging from the sinking sun, it was late afternoon.

He grabbed a thick slice of bread from the bread box and absentmindedly ripped off a bite as he plopped down on a chair, carefully spreading out the papers before him. There wasn't a lot here on Miss DeVries. It looked like it had been collected in a hurry with a lot of obvious gaps.

She was twenty years old and apparently had had a few run-ins with the law as well. Though nothing too serious was listed, it was readily apparent this was one troubled young lady. He looked for the obvious clues first.

Divorced parents? Nope. They were both listed here. Curtis and Rachel DeVries.

History of past abuse? Nothing was indicated.

Spiritual background? Ah — here might be something. According to the forms filled out by her parents, they'd accepted Jesus Christ as their Savior only about four or five years ago. He digested that for a moment. It wouldn't have been the first time he'd seen a kid who rebelled at the sudden change in their house when their parents "found God." A definite maybe there.

Siblings? Listed was one sister. Yvonne. Didn't list an age. He flipped through more of the sheets. Curiously absent was any other information regarding the sister — however old she was. Older? Younger?

He looked again.

Nope. There were pages on Curtis.

Rachel. The brief one on Carillon.

No Yvonne anywhere else.

Maybe she was married and gone or something.

A sudden knock at his door made him jump. Straightening the papers, he rose and pulled open the heavy door. In the growing twilight stood Steve again, this time accompanied by Bob and a few others of the full-time staff of Yesteryear. Their faces were far from comfortable.

"W–what is it?" Jack asked.

Steve was the first to respond. "Remember that girl you were working on reassigning? Carillon DeVries?"

He nodded.

"Well," his friend continued, "Ruth had that talk with her. I guess it didn't go too well."

That didn't sound too unusual. Ordinarily those types were prone to argue. "And?" Jack prompted.

"We need your help." He threw Jack a flashlight. "She's come up missing."

Carillon kept walking. Trying to ignore the mosquitos that were conveniently making her their supper. Trying to ignore the odd noises that ricocheted through the dense trees. Trying to ignore the growing dark and the fact that she had no clue where she was — much less any experience about guiding herself through the middle of no-where. To call her a city girl would have been an understatement.

There were some things she did know, however. Namely that these people here, these "God" people, were no different from her parents and all their flaky friends from their church. In their eyes she could do no right. Ever.

She'd been stupid to stay even one night. She should have left yesterday — right away. When she'd had more time. When she could still see. The ever-growing dark-ness was getting more than intimidating now. She was afraid.

"Come on, Carillon," she whispered. "You can get out of here. You can find someplace. Some sort of road. Anything."

But it seemed that each step took her only deeper into unforgiving thickets of briars and branches that held all their secrets silent. The woods weren't going to tell her anything.

Then a new thought captured her and took her hostage.

This was it. This was the end.

This was her punishment. For what she'd done to Evie.

Backing herself against the rough bark of a tree, she leaned against it, her chest heaving with each ragged, painful breath. There was nowhere to go. Nowhere to hide.

Part of her wanted to sit down right there — to just give up. Give in. It was what she deserved.

But another part, unknown to her until now, urged her stumbling feet forward, willing her self-preservation. She gasped and charged blindly through the wicked branches that left their bloody mark across her face and neck and arms. And she ran. From herself. And from the demons she'd learned would never leave her alone — until they had her for themselves.

# Chapter 5

They were getting close. Jack could tell. This part of the woods would never be foreign to him. It held too many memories. Too many ghosts.

For tonight he was thankful to have another reason to be out here. A different reason to trail through the darkened, tree-studded, and overgrown paths.

In the distance, he could hear the others' faint voices. "Carillon!" Her name echoed through the branches and across the night sky. Jack knew it was useless for him to try and call out anything. He'd have to rely on other means.

*Father . . . You see her. You know exactly where she is. Keep her safe, Lord. And lead me to her.*

That prayer internally voiced, he forged on, trying to be sensitive to the Holy Spirit's leading.

Carillon sat in utter fear and misery, the damp, cold ground stealing her warmth, her security.

Her eyes shut tightly, she could hear nothing. She could see nothing. Nothing but the memories that kept swaying across her memory in a haunting waltz. . . .

"Tony, stop it," she heard herself laughing.

His disarming grin was all he needed. "Come on, your parents aren't home yet." His lips reclaimed her neck, making her squirm in pleasure.

"Knock it off." She pushed him away halfheartedly. "They aren't home. But my little sister's upstairs."

"Asleep," he reminded her as his hands started their familiar foray again.

"Tony," she murmured, fully enjoying the whole forbidden aspect of his being there.

That's when he stopped.

"Did you hear that?" he asked, frowning in concentration.

Carillon laughed. "Hear what?" She listened for a moment, then giggled once more. "Now you're paranoid, Mister. Come on. . . ." She invited his attentions, enjoying baiting him again and again.

He kissed her somewhat distractedly.

She slumped against the back of the couch and glared at him. "What is your problem?"

"Lon, I'm serious. I think I heard something."

"My parents are not home."

"Not that. Something else."

She slid him a look out of the corner of her eye and smiled slyly. "All right. Fine. I'll go up and see if Evie is spying on us if you're so convinced." She heaved herself up from the leather sofa and straightened her rumpled T-shirt before heading toward the stairs. "But you'd better still be here when I come back down."

"Oh, I will." His seductive smile promised nothing less than that.

Carillon took the stairs two at a time, the sound of her footsteps lost in the plush carpet. She was in a hurry. Check on Evie, close her door tighter, and get back down to Tony before her parents got home.

As she approached the end of the hall, she saw her sister's door was open a crack, just as she'd left it after tucking her in. She started to turn around, certain that nothing or no one had moved since her last trip upstairs.

But something made her decide to peek in — just to make sure.

Easing the door open, she let her eyes wander across the six-year-old's room, the floor strewn with a jungle of stuffed animals, each creature subtly illuminated by the bedside nightlight.

A familiar lump was buried under the pale pink comforter. Carillon smiled. How the kid could sleep with her head totally covered was beyond her. She slipped into the room, just to adjust the blankets around the sleeping form.

She gently pulled back the hem of the comforter, anticipating her baby sister's angelic face reposed in sleep.

Two large, black, unblinking eyes stared back.

Carillon gasped and jumped back.

Then laughed.

Stealthily waiting under the covers was none other than Riley — Evie's overgrown, overstuffed, over-loved brown teddy bear. She tossed him aside and felt around the bed clothes for her sister.

Nothing.

Great. She was supposed to be sleeping . . . and she was probably hiding out in her walk-in closet playing with Barbies — as usual. "Evie?" She started toward the closet door. "Come on, Bug. You're supposed to be asleep."

The door was shut fast.

She yanked on the knob, awaiting her sister's shocked look upon discovery.

The closet was black.

Carillon reached over and flicked on the switch.

Nothing.

Every blouse, every toy was in its place. None telling any secrets.

An uncontrollable panic seized Carillon. She ran back into the hallway and yelled down the stairs. "Tony! Tony, get up here!"

His tall, broad form lumbered into view, the confusion evident on his handsome face. "Yeah, what?"

She gulped. "She's not here. Evie's gone."

The cold was back again. At least she could feel it. Hugging her legs to her chest, Carillon edged herself closer to the tree trunk and rocked slowly back and forth. Trying to stay warm. Trying to forget. Trying to pretend she was somewhere else — someone else. Away from all the things that haunted her no matter where she went. Even here . . . in the middle of nowhere.

They were all around. She could hear them taunting her. It was only a matter of time before they reached out to take her. Only when her resolve was just weak enough.

"Oh, Evie," she whispered through numb

lips. "I'm so sorry. . . ."

The lightest of sensations brushed across her arm.

With a petrified scream, she tried to leap to her feet, only to find herself tangled up with some wicked vine. It sent her crashing to the soggy earth again.

Then the light hit her, blinding her momentarily before it slid away.

Still trying to adjust to the spots in her eyes and her erratic breathing, she shielded her eyes from glare and watched as the beam swung up and around.

It illuminated those eyes. The kind eyes. The ones like Evie's.

"Are y–y–you . . . all . . . right?" His voice was barely above a whisper, but it echoed through the stillness around her. And she felt them flee — all the things that had been hounding her and haunting her.

She nodded slowly, wiping her sleeve under her nose.

His hand reached out to her. Sure. Unthreatening.

Hesitating for a split second, she finally relented and grasped it in turn. It's warmth and strength surprised her. He helped pull her to her feet and, once again, slid his own warm wraps around her shoulders.

Without another word, he led her through

the maze of tangled limbs and branches. Leaving Carillon to wonder what on earth she had done to deserve being saved.

He hadn't seen her since that night. Well, only in passing. She seemed to be avoiding him — if he was guessing right. Why? That he didn't know. There was a lot more to Miss Carillon DeVries than she was letting on — of that he was sure. But in the end, he reminded himself, it wasn't really his concern or his business. He'd not let himself get wrapped up in any fantasy like that again. He'd just do his job.

The last aspect of his job, relating to her anyway, was her new placement at the Mitchell House, the historic home located in the little section of Yesteryear called Liberty Town. It was, without question, the largest and most well-appointed house on the grounds. The gentleman, Ambrose Mitchell, who'd founded the sawmill, had built the place in the mid-1800s. Not much was spared in its construction. And while by today's standards of a mansion, it wasn't a huge place, it was large enough — with enough antiques to make even the most experienced collector a little green with envy.

Miss DeVries's new job as a "maid" at the Mitchell House seemed like a suitable match. It didn't require her to deal with the public in any sort of interactive way; it kept her in a place where there were a lot of people, lest she try and run off again. And it kept her busy with light duties of cleaning and other appropriate tasks suited to the era of the home.

It was three days into the placement, and so far, so good. Everything else at Yesteryear seemed to be running like a well-oiled machine. Jack was in Bob's office, going over the plans for the annual employee picnic they held at the lake the beginning of every summer. They were just about to discuss the merits of renting some rowboats when the door flew open.

Betty Haskins, the older woman in charge of collecting, cataloging, and caring for the numerous antiques at the variety of sites, pushed into the room, her eyes ablaze. "I tried to overlook it for awhile, Bob. Thought it might have been coincidence. But no longer. She has got to go!"

Bob raised his brows and exchanged a look with Jack. "Uh, have a seat, Betty."

She lowered her reed-slim frame into the wooden chair, her back stiff as a ramrod.

"What seems to be the problem?"

"That DeVries girl! She's robbing us blind!"

Jack felt his heart sink, and he released a slow breath, trying to ignore Bob's second glance at him.

"Slow down, Betty. Why don't you start from the beginning?"

"Well, as you know, we have that wonderful set of Spode china in the Mitchells' cabinet. In addition to the silver service and place setting that are under the glass case."

Bob nodded.

"There are pieces missing."

"How many?"

"Three cups and saucers, the sugar and creamer set, and at least half a dozen of the utensils." She threw an accusatory glare at Jack. "And it's been since she's been there."

"You can't go accusing people until we know for sure," Bob patiently reminded the pinched-faced woman. "Are you sure they haven't simply been misplaced?"

She looked highly offended. "They are nowhere to be found. They are gone. Only I have the key to those cupboards. And only the maid staff has access to my office." She nodded as if that settled the whole issue. Her attention fell back on Jack, and her eyes all but dared him with the unspoken question: *What are you going to do about it?*

"All right, Betty," Bob said on a sigh. "Thank you for bringing this to our attention. We'll look into it."

She rose abruptly from her chair. "Shall I begin filling out the insurance paperwork?"

Bob and Jack exchanged looks again.

"No," the older man said. "Let's hold off awhile. Just to see if anything turns up."

She still didn't leave. After a long silence, she piped up again. "And what about her?"

Bob tried to look busy with paperwork. "Jack will look into it."

She looked doubtful, but turned and whisked out the door with her usual efficiency, closing it tightly behind her.

Jack slunk back against the wall and rubbed his suddenly tired eyes.

Bob looked at him with raised brows. He didn't need to ask.

"I–I–I'll go . . . t–t–talk to . . . her."

Bob nodded. "Let me know how it goes." He returned his attention to his desk, obviously relieved not to have to deal with these sticky personnel issues.

The walk from Bob's office to Liberty Town took Jack only about five minutes — not nearly enough time for him to compile any sort of plan as to what he would say or ask of the young woman.

The familiar clangs of iron upon iron came from Paul's blacksmith shop, the smell of hot metal wafting out on the early

63

summer breeze. Jack wished he had a moment to stop and talk to his friend — he was always full of good, godly counsel. But based on Betty's present state of mind, he thought he'd better get this done.

He marched past the small church, the general store, the inn, and a variety of other houses, slowly approaching the Mitchell House, which lay at the end of the short, dusty main street. Out in the yard, he saw Carla hanging the feather pillows on the line, beating them with the iron tool designed for the task of airing and cleaning the plump, white bags. She smiled warmly at Jack. "Morning," she said.

He nodded in return. "D–do you know . . . where I–I — can . . . fffind —"

"Miss DeVries?" she finished for him.

Jack nodded. It wasn't unusual for people to try and finish his sentences for him. In the beginning it had irritated him. But as he grew older, he realized they were only trying to help. The only time it caused problems was when they totally guessed wrong at the outcome of the sentence he was trying to utter. But he usually managed to get his point across.

Today, Carla already knew.

He nodded again.

"She's upstairs, making the beds, I think."

He smiled a thank-you and headed toward the rear entrance of the two-story white house. It was unusually quiet in the kitchen. Lynette, the house cook, who was normally in a bubbly mood, merely nodded at him over the pot of soup she was stirring as he passed through. He guessed that the whole house was in a state of discomfort due to the current circumstances.

With another sigh, he ascended the servant's steep stairs leading from the kitchen to the upstairs bedrooms. In the main hallway, he noticed the breeze wafting in, airing out the stale smell of the old house. From down the corridor, he heard the shuffling sounds of feet on the hardwood floor.

Breathing a quick prayer for wisdom and direction, he started down the hall. She was in the second bedroom, carefully making the bed. Really carefully.

He wasn't sure what it was, but something made him stop, unnoticed, and just watch her for a time.

As she stood in the middle of the bedroom that had belonged to Ambrose Mitchell's young daughter, surrounded by a wooden rocking horse and an assortment of faded china dolls, she almost looked like a little girl herself.

Moving around with a quiet air, she

tucked each corner of the intricately stitched quilt firmly into place around the sleigh bed's ornate head and footboard. Then she scooped up a handful of crude stuffed animals made from old flannel with spare buttons for eyes and gently, but methodically, placed them at the head of the bed, right in front of the recently fluffed pillows.

She stepped back and stared at them for a time. Silent.

Her face wasn't visible . . . and he wished he could see some sort of expression. Some reason for her unlikely attention to this little detail.

Finally, his conscience got the better of him. Before she turned around and actually caught him staring, he thought he'd better make his presence known.

Shuffling his feet, he cleared his throat as though he'd just happened upon the scene.

She whirled around a little too quickly. Like she'd been caught at something. And then her expression changed — like she'd just seen a ghost. Almost the way she'd looked when he'd found her that night in the woods.

But the look disappeared quickly. Just as it had that night once they'd come back to the compound. There'd been no thank-you.

No gratitude. No words at all. She'd simply walked into her room and shut the door.

"Yes?" she asked him, the hesitation in her voice obvious.

"C–could I–I–I sssp— Could . . . I–I– . . . talk . . . to you?"

A hardness fell across her delicate features. Her back stiffened. Smoothing out the black skirt of her maid's uniform, she stepped purposefully toward the door, brushed past him, and headed down the stairs.

At first he thought she was just leaving. Period. He double-timed it down the steps after her but slowed when he saw her out the kitchen window, waiting in the corner of the yard by the white-picket fence.

Lynette, the cook, gave him another odd look as he passed by the stove. He ignored it this time and headed straight for Carillon. Her back was toward him, as she faced the small village's freshly planted fields just beyond them.

"They think I took them, don't they?" Her voice was quiet and strong all at the same time.

Jack dug the toe of his work boot into the dusty dirt beneath the grass. "I–i–it ssseems . . . that . . . way."

She turned around. Jack was surprised to

find a hint of redness in her deep-set blue eyes. "I know. I've heard the other girls talking." She crossed her arms and let out a long, frustrated breath.

"D–d–did . . . you?" He knew he had to ask, in spite of the discomfort it caused him.

She leveled a disdainful glare at him. "No."

Jack nodded and cleared his throat, wondering how to go about this next part.

"But," she jumped in instead, almost as if reading his thoughts, "that doesn't matter, does it?"

He slowly shook his head. "I–I–I'm afraid not. F–f–for now . . . I'll h–h–have to . . . move you . . . ssssomeplace . . . else."

She began to untie the lacy white apron covering her skirt, yanking the strings more forcefully than necessary. "Fine." She threw the apron over the nearby fence. "Where do I get banished to now?"

Jack ran his hand through his hair. Man, this was a lot harder than usual. "I–I'll have to t–to get . . . back t–t–to you."

"Why?" she yelled, seeming to suddenly explode. "Why am I even here? No one likes me. No one wants me here. No one believes me! What do I have to do or say to make you understand?"

He rubbed uncomfortably at his jaw,

unsure how to handle this little outburst.

"Don't you understand?" she asked again. She moved in closer. "Here, decipher this." Her eyes took on a hard edginess. "I–I–I," she stammered, "d–d–didn't . . . t–t–take the sssstupid c–c–c–cups!"

Jack knew he willed his face not to change expression. He'd had enough practice at that. All the way through school as a kid. Even into adulthood. But he also knew he couldn't will away the fraction of his soul that wilted every time it happened. And this time especially. What was it about this woman that made him so sensitive . . . ? *God, give me patience. Give me Your patience. Your grace.*

He stood his ground and waited for her tirade to end.

Nothing else came.

"I–I–I'll . . . meet you . . . at the m–m–main office. One hour."

He turned and walked away, wondering if she'd even show up.

# Chapter 6

Well, she surprised him. She actually showed up.

Her face was still unreadable, and Jack couldn't help but assume that she'd made it her life's work perfecting that nonchalance. But he also knew there was something else there. Something of which he'd seen only a glimpse — but it was there nonetheless.

Still smarting somewhat from her earlier imitation, he found it a little easier to erect a more objective frame of mind and a professional attitude. Now, if only his ridiculous speech would allow him some reprieve. . . .

They were in Bob's office, Carillon seated haphazardly in the small chair in front of the desk. Jack stood off to one side of the overloaded desk of papers — preferring not to take the seat in any "authoritative, dictatorial" position. And as long as he had the papers in his hands, he might as well get this done.

"Th–th–there is . . . one p–p–position left. . . ."

"Cleaning toilets?" she asked smartly.

He ignored the comment.

"A sssssschool. Y–you . . . w–w–would be . . . the . . . t–t–t–teacher."

"A teacher?" The level of surprise in her voice nearly matched the arch of her back as she straightened up quickly. "Like, with kids?"

"Ssssssort of."

Her head shook vehemently. "I don't think that's such a good —"

He halted her protest with an upraised index finger. "Not . . . k–kids all . . . th–th–the . . . time. Only . . . ssssspecial days."

She settled back in the chair slightly, but the frown didn't leave her heart-shaped face.

"Y–y–you'll m–mostly . . . give . . . t–t–tours of . . . the . . . sssssschool to . . . visitors." He hoped that was clear enough. In addition, he'd written out what the expectations were for the role of the small town's "schoolmarm." It was easier than his trying to stutter through the whole scenario. He handed her the papers . . . and waited.

Was it his imagination, or did her hands shake ever so slightly as she took them?

"Where is the school?" she asked after a long silence. "I don't recall seeing it in the town."

"I–it's a . . . ways . . . out. P–p–past the . . . fff–farm . . . fields."

Again, she sat in obvious mute misery.

He felt like he needed to say something. But what?

With a long sigh, she stood from the chair and turned toward the door. "Well, thanks so much." The derision in her tone was less than subtle.

"I–I–I'm . . . sssssssorry. Ab–bout . . . the . . . l–l–last job."

She turned back toward him. "Are you?" She huffed in disbelief. "I find that a little hard to believe. It seems everyone around here is just glad to be rid of me. Why should you be any different?"

Jack swallowed and glanced at his boots before returning a concerned look. He shrugged. "I . . . hope I . . . am."

"Right." She leaned toward the awaiting door again.

*Say something,* an unprompted voice urged him. *Go ahead . . . mention it.* He frowned at the odd direction, but delved in anyway.

"Sssssome . . . day," he interrupted her escape, "I–I'd like . . . t–t–to hear about . . . y–your ssssister."

She froze in her tracks.

It was some time before she actually

turned back toward him.

When she finally did, her face was a mixture of shock, anger, and . . . guilt?

"How did you know about my sister?" she asked, her voice barely above a whisper.

He nodded toward the file on the desk. "Y–y–your . . . file."

Her eyes narrowed as she threw a penetrating gaze toward the brown case. "What did it say?"

He picked up the papers and flipped through them. "Just . . . th–th–that you . . . have a sssssister." He looked at the sheet again. "Yvonne?"

Her face paled at the mention of the name.

Something inside of Jack clicked with realization.

This was it.

This was the reason for her being here. For her surliness. For that tough facade that she'd managed to create over . . . whatever it was.

Gripping her handful of papers until her knuckles turned white, she wrenched open the door and purposefully walked out of the office, leaving the door agape behind her.

And leaving Jack to wonder all the more. What was that pain behind her clouded eyes?

Without a moment's hesitation, he

scanned the file once more and found it. Phone number. He sat down at Bob's desk and lifted the receiver from the cradle.

Carillon took her time walking from the office back through Liberty Town. Indeed, it seemed as if her feet were on autopilot. They had to have been because her mind was certainly nowhere on her surroundings.

He knew about Evie. But how much? And how many others knew?

No wonder they wanted her out of every place he tried to place her. . . . She was a danger — out and out.

She'd already passed by the majority of the places on Main Street when she began to round the corner around Mitchell House. Her thoughts temporarily withdrawn from the past, she noticed several of the maids trying not to peer too obviously in her direction. They were doing a lousy job at it. The only one who seemed to be paying her absolutely no mind at all was the cook — she busily kept digging around in the fenced garden, her head never lifting once.

Carillon was secretly grateful.

Once she'd passed the perimeter of the yard, she gathered herself together enough to glance at the papers Jack had given her. There was supposed to be a map marking the spot of the school in relation to Liberty Town.

Jack.

If her mind had not been in such an upheaval, she might have laughed at the thought of him. Of her. Here she'd gone and pinned her hopes of escape on that young man. How far had that gotten her? Walking from Liberty Town to a remote schoolhouse — that's where.

Training her mind away from the disturbing mention of her sister, she tried to formulate a new plan. A new plan for getting out of here. Maybe this new posting was her unencumbered escape in hiding.

No people around.

Plenty of time to scout out the surrounding area — so she'd not be caught in the woods like the last time.

No, this could well be it. All she had to do was be patient. Be patient — and think. Think hard. She could — no, she would get herself out of this. Once and for all.


Jack didn't hear him enter.

He still sat at the desk. His head in his hands. The folder in front of him. His thoughts in an unusual mess.

"Jack?"

Bob's low voice startled him back to reality. He jerked up his head and dropped his hands onto the papers before him.

"Everything all right?" The older man's whiskered face registered immediate concern as he hung up his hat and sat in the remaining small chair.

Jack jumped up, pushing the papers quickly together. "Sssssssorry. Here's . . . your . . . ch–ch–chair."

Bob waved it off, but the worry didn't leave his eyes. "What's up?"

Jack finished collecting the file and tapped it smartly against the metal desk. "I–I–I'm not . . . sure."

His boss remained pensive. "Does it have something to do with Miss DeVries?"

A nod.

"She didn't take the news well?"

He shrugged. "About . . . h–h–h–how I . . . g–guessed . . . she would."

"But?"

Jack frowned and bit on his lower lip for a moment, trying to form some sort of response. One that might make sense . . . even when none of it did to him yet. "Th–th–there's ssssomething . . . else. Why . . . she's . . . here." He let out a long breath. "I . . . almost . . . c–c–called her . . . p–p–parents. To . . . ffff–find out . . . ssssome . . . things."

"Almost?"

He shook his head. "Couldn't. Sssssomething . . . told me . . . n–not to."

"Something?" Bob cocked his head in curiosity. "Or Someone?"

Jack gave him a halfhearted grin. "Rrrr–right."

The older man eased up from the chair and rounded the desk, clapping a huge supportive hand on Jack's shoulder. "Well, then, Jack, I'd say you're on the right track. You usually have a pretty keen sense about these things."

He shot him a doubtful look.

"Well . . . you with some help from the Lord then."

This time he nodded.

As Bob took his seat, Jack headed for the door, beginning again to try to sort out the whole situation.

"Jack?"

He turned back, brows raised in question.

Bob's large, round fingers kneaded his glistening forehead for a second or two. "There is some concern — among the other staff members."

Jack turned fully around.

"They're questioning the wisdom of placing Miss DeVries in such a remote spot."

"W–w–well . . . they . . . d–didn't want . . .

her w–w–w–with others."

"True, true. But they're worrying more about another escape attempt. Or her trying to stash more things she might have taken."

Unaccountably, Jack bristled. "Sh–sh–she d–didn't . . . take . . . those."

The man's eyebrows rose a fraction. "Are you sure?"

Shuffling his feet, Jack swallowed hard. "No . . . proof. B–but I . . . j–j–just know."

"I see." He folded his hands together patiently. "Any idea where those things disappeared to then?"

Jack shook his head miserably.

"What about the other concern? Her possible future attempts to run off? Do you have any 'feelings' along that line?"

Again, he had to indicate that he didn't know.

"Jack," Bob began — he was using that professional voice he got when he was overly concerned about something. "I'm going to give this about a week. If she can prove that she can stick to this and doesn't cause any more problems, I'll let her stay. Otherwise, you know what our choices are."

This time Jack nodded. He knew. He'd seen it done. Not often, but done nonetheless.

He just hated to think of Carillon as being

that kind of troublemaker. There was a definite reason she was supposed to be here. He knew it. He could feel it. If only he could help her find it.

"That's it," Bob said quietly.

Shaking himself out of his reverie, Jack shifted the file in his arms and nodded.

He turned and left. His heart . . . heavy.

Her legs were already tired, and the mosquitoes were starting to get downright vicious. Carillon kept trudging through the knee-high grasses, the path to wherever she was going long since lost in the disuse of the place.

Several minutes later, she saw it.

A small clearing amid a stand of trees. Two small, white buildings looking lonely and forlorn. Brushing a strand of hair out of her eyes, she looked on in chagrin. Then she turned and looked behind her. Liberty Town was out of sight, the path disappearing around the stand of woods curving off to her right.

With a long sigh, she faced the bleak-looking picture before her. The schoolhouse was obviously the bigger of the two . . . a large set of double doors fronting the entrance. The other, smaller, square construction sat fifty feet or so from the school.

And this was . . . ?

Carillon glanced through the papers Jack had given her once more. Where was that map? The directions? Nearly losing her grip as she simultaneously sorted papers and swatted at persistent mosquitoes, she at last found the page.

Sure enough. Two buildings were indicated.

One schoolhouse.

One teacherage.

Teacherage?

What on earth was a teacherage . . . ?

A sudden yip and howl from somewhere entirely too close echoed in her ear, sending a blood-chilling shiver down her spine.

Tripping over her own feet in clumsy fear, Carillon ran to the smaller of the two outposts.

Another yip, from somewhere slightly farther off, answered the first.

By the time she reached the small door, she was completely out of breath and her heart was racing so fast it hurt. Knowing no greater relief than when the knob turned under her hand, she slipped into the little house and slammed the door behind her.

The next few eternal seconds were spent trying to catch her breath, slow down her racing pulse, and carefully listening for any more unfamiliar and unwelcome sounds from outside.

None seemed to come.

Allowing herself a slight breath of respite, she took a moment to take in the decor of the one-room building.

It was obviously a living quarters.

And it had obviously been visited recently. Funny she hadn't noticed any tracks through that long grass. . . .

Even so, the small bed was crisply made with a rustic quilt and fresh white sheets. On one side of the bed stood an old ladder-back chair. Above it were several hooks hanging at different intervals on the rough planked wall — apparently her closet.

She turned and assessed the remainder of the small room. Two windows flanked the east and west walls. In the opposite corner stood an old woodstove, a fresh pile of firewood stacked neatly by its side. A small sideboard that must have done double duty as a cupboard and a sink with the graniteware tub on top of it. Closer to her, a rather rickety-looking table, recently laden with fresh bread, cheese, and a pitcher of water, and two more ladder-back chairs completed the furnishings. In their entirety.

No bathroom.

She'd kind of expected that. But to have

to trek to an outhouse when she was way out —

The high-pitched yipping ricocheted about her again.

Suddenly overcome with fear and complete misery, Carillon sat on the edge of the bed, her nails digging into the thin mattress. She'd never felt so alone . . . In a split second her tortured thoughts flew to Evie. Was this how she had felt? Had she been this afraid? Felt this alone?

Unbidden, the tears began to trail down her cheeks, the first in a long, long time. "Oh, Evie," she whispered to the silence. "I'm so sorry. I'm so sorry I wasn't there for you . . . when I should have been." The sobs caught in her throat, making it ache in a way it never had before.

All Carillon could do was to lie down on the wind-dried quilt and let the consuming tears keep flowing. There was no stopping them. No stopping the pain.

All she knew was that she wanted to die.

# Chapter 7

Sutter's Lake was really more of a glorified pond. But it was cold, and wet, and welcome on humid summer days like this one. Jack helped unload the last of the canoes, setting them along the sandy edge of the brownish water. The June day was shaping up into a hot one already, and he was finally beginning to have hope that the crops might be all right.

In between all those thoughts and his own chores at the farmstead where he stayed, his mind kept racing back to Carillon DeVries. On the guise of readying the schoolhouse for the next week's visitors, he trekked over to her area almost daily. In truth there was a lot that needed doing on the old building.

But in all his trips and work around it, he'd yet to see her.

Well, up close anyway.

On a few occasions he'd get the distinct feeling that he was being watched. He'd nonchalantly step back down the ladder to retrieve more nails for his pouch or something and casually slide a glance toward the teacherage. A flicker of movement at the window was all he'd glimpse. She never came out. Never spoke to him. Nothing.

But she'd also not caused any more problems . . . that he'd heard about. Bob seemed to have forgotten about the threatening prospect of sending her away. Inwardly Jack was relieved — he still sensed that urgency from within. She needed to be here. But mingled with that relief was trepidation — a feeling his flesh knew too well by now. That part of him still ached at the bitterness and resentment she seemed to harbor toward him. And he was at a loss as to why . . . or what to do about it.

In the end, he did all he knew to do. He gave it to God and prayed that even if he never uncovered the reason, she'd know His peace. Somehow. Sometime.

"Jack!" A voice carried across the small body of water.

He glanced up from straightening the last canoe and waved at Carla, the Mitchell House maid.

"Save me a ride, okay?"

He grinned and sent her an informal salute. It had become a yearly tradition since Carla had started working at Yesteryear. They'd trek out in the water one last time before the boats were all loaded up. He wasn't sure how it started or why . . . but they always had a nice time. Sometimes chatting amiably, other times just sitting in companionable silence.

Of all the young women at Yesteryear, Carla was the only one with whom Jack felt somewhat comfortable. Maybe it was because she'd looked past his stutter from the first moment they'd met, whereas with the others, they took on that familiar discomfort until they'd gotten to know him well.

She was also, as a fellow farm kid, one of the few people who understood his frustrations that seemed to resurface regularly — especially in the springtime. It never failed. As soon as the spring sunshine would hit the black earth, sending the lingering aroma wafting around on the light breezes, it would come. That old desire.

To turn over the earth and plant a new seed. To begin anew.

To see it grow, green and proud.

To harvest it at its fruition.

To take the bounty from God's creation and make it a living.

Even now he sighed at the memory. In spite of the fact that it had been nearly ten years since he'd actively farmed, he could remember every nuance, every chore, every sensation related to each aspect of the life.

It wasn't a place he usually dwelt on long, though. For with those fond memories came also the not so fond. The pain. The loneliness. The despair. The sheer disappointment . . . in himself and in his family.

"Hey, Jack!" Paul was headed in his direction.

Jack looked up, grateful for the mental intrusion, and smiled at his friend. He fought another pang of temporary envy as he watched the towering, muscular form of the blacksmith striding toward him, clad only in his swim trunks.

He had no reason to harbor grudging feelings toward the man. Paul had never lorded his size over Jack or anyone else. It was just one more issue that seemed to creep up when Jack's memories were centered on his past.

He tried not to think about his feelings as he straightened his T-shirt over his own slim frame and clasped Paul's hand in a friendly grip. "Rrrr–ready . . . for a . . . sssswim I . . . see."

"You got it! Where's everybody else?"

Jack shrugged. "Sssssstill b–b–bringing the . . . food . . . I guess."

"Awesome! I'm starved." Paul grinned and immediately began slipping off his tennis shoes. Two seconds later, the tall blond was cavorting in the water, yelling for some of the others approaching to join him.

It wasn't long before the entire assembly of Yesteryear's workers and employees joined each other around the quietly lapping shores of Sutter's Lake. The gathering marked the beginning of their summer season — one filled with hard work, new beginnings, new friendships, and a lot of growth for many of those in attendance.

Jack couldn't help but smile as he watched several of the newcomers laughing around the smattering of picnic tables. Already healing had begun. It was the primary purpose of Yesteryear, one in which he couldn't deny his pride. If it could help only a few . . . just to keep those hurts from sprouting into long-term hardships. And ending in a tragic situation like that of his older brother, Jon.

The mere thought of his brother brought back a host of different visions, none of which were too appealing. He shook his head. If only there'd been a place like Yesteryear for Jon. And his father.

Carillon had gotten brave enough over the past few days to actually leave the front door of her little house open. The stifling air swarming around its small interior was too overwhelming without some fresh breeze. But there was no question as to when it got shut. As soon as dusk threatened on the western horizon, the wood-paneled door would be latched securely — heat and humidity or not. No wolves were going to get her.

She'd already lost count of the days while being in this isolated spot. The only things that seemed to divide her awareness of the times were Jack's regular, daily visits to the schoolhouse. To her surprise, he never approached her new little home, instead keeping himself busy hammering, nailing, repairing, and cleaning up in general around the little school.

An unaccountable shyness had prevented her from saying anything to him, either. She couldn't quite place her finger on it. At first, she thought it was merely the anger and frustration she'd felt toward all the people who seemed determined to get her.

But if she were to be totally honest with herself, she somehow knew she couldn't blame him for any of that. He'd just been doing his job when he'd reassigned her here.

Then there was the issue of those eyes. Those golden brown pools of emotion that held the uncanny ability to look straight through her. Too scary.

She knew her plan to figure out the layout of this place and all its surrounding land needed to be dealt with soon — before she lost her nerve. But realizing that in Jack Tate lay the only accessible resource for doing so, she found herself putting it off. She needed to steel herself.

So while she waited for that to happen, she took some opportunities to poke around in the schoolhouse when he'd left after his few hours' work. The wood floor, swept clean, supported a handful of simple wooden benches and crude desks. An over-sized map of the state of Wisconsin hung on the otherwise sparsely occupied wall. A meager blackboard flanked it on one side, her own small teacher's desk on the other.

The outstanding feature in the one-room school was the huge wood-burning stove, its long black pipe snaking upward and then across the length of the rectangular room. Carillon, more than once, was incredibly grateful that it wasn't the season where she needed to feed the thing. She'd already discovered that nuisance in her own dwelling. After countless burned fingers and nearly smoking herself out of the place, she decided she could live on sandwich makings alone. Hot food, at the moment, was over-rated.

But the most unusual find didn't come until the second or third day. And she hadn't even been looking for it.

She'd gone to hang up one of her new "schoolteacher" dresses on the hooks beside her bed. To her amazement, it fell to the floor. Not just the dress, but the whole hook — and a small portion of the paneling behind it.

Berating herself for having already made a mess that would need repair, probably by Jack, she picked up the chunk of wood, determined to refasten it somehow on her own.

That's when she saw them.

Between the inner and outer walls, lying snugly against a board, were two very old, very dusty, leather-bound books.

Curious, she slid her hand into the thin opening, wrinkling her nose when a handful of cobwebs followed. Gently cleaning off the covers, she stared at the ancient volumes, intrigued.

Easing open one of the fragile covers, she squinted at the faded blue script:

*Madeline Whitcomb*
*15 August 1853*

Obviously some sort of journal. Carillon

flipped through the pages. A good many of them were filled. August, into September . . . she scanned the end. The last entry was from the beginning of June of the next year.

Laying it aside, she picked up the second little book. The cracked and faded black leather felt rough under her fingertips. Aged gold lettering centered the front cover: Holy Bible.

With a frown, she laid it back on the table. And stared at it for awhile. The old feelings of anger and inadequacy surfaced.

If it hadn't been such a ridiculous notion, she might have attributed its presence there to her parents. But that was ridiculous. They hadn't known where she was going. Where she'd be.

Nonetheless, she pushed the book farther back on the table and picked up the journal. With nothing else to fill her time, this looked the more interesting of the two volumes.

But if Carillon thought she was going to get away from God or religion, she was mistaken. Apparently, Miss Whitcomb, whom she discovered to have been the teacher at this very school in 1853, proved to be more than religious herself. More often than not, her entries were feelings, thoughts, poetry, and prayers all mingled together.

Carillon might have set it aside were it not

for the intriguing manner of the woman's observations on other matters.

The teacher, whatever her age might have been, obviously had been lonely. To deal with her feelings of isolation, Madeline had listed several Scripture verses. Tempted to skip over the words initially, Carillon found herself going back and reading them anyway — simply because of the soothing effect they seemed to have had on Miss Whitcomb's later entries:

*He shall not be afraid of evil tidings: his heart is fixed, trusting in the Lord.* (Psalm 112:7)

*Fear thou not; for I am with thee: be not dismayed; for I am thy God; I will strengthen thee; yea, I will help thee; yea, I will uphold thee with the right hand of my righteousness.* (Isaiah 41:10)

*The Lord is my strength and my shield; my heart trusted in Him, and I am helped: therefore my heart greatly rejoiceth; and with my song will I praise Him.* (Psalm 28:7)

Carillon read the words with a distant, skeptical interest. Partially because of the sheer engaging personality of the woman who wrote it . . . and partially because, for some weird reason, it made Carillon think of Evie.

Even more strange, her fear of the loneliness that had enveloped her the first day or so had gradually given way to some bizarre form of exhaustion. She found herself sleeping more often than not. And while the nightmares and visions of Evie still floated through her mind, she was able to awaken and for the first time in a long time differentiate between her present surroundings and the awful places of the past.

Yet it was one of those places that kept her at the teacherage today — when she knew full well the others were having their picnic at a nearby lake. That was a place where she needn't go. Ever. No matter what Madeline Whitcomb said about her "strength."

"I'll just wait here," Carla offered.

Jack turned back from his trek through the tall grass, his look questioning. "You . . . sure?"

She nodded as she glanced over his shoulder at the schoolhouse. "I don't think she likes me much."

Jack had to chuckle, in spite of it all. "Sh–sh–she . . . doesn't . . . l–like me . . . much . . . either."

Carla still shrugged. "You go ahead. I'll wait here until you get back."

He tilted his head in acquiescence and proceeded toward the small building.

He wasn't looking forward to this. At all. It had been Bob's idea to send him over to check on Miss DeVries, since she'd flatly declined the invitation to join the others this afternoon.

Expecting the door might be slammed in his face — if she opened it at all — he took a deep breath and stepped onto the small stoop. He rapped his knuckles on the door frame and tried to think of what he might say if she answered.

He didn't have much time.

The door squeaked open fairly quickly, and her blue eyes peered out at him, full of questions and curiosity. "Yes?"

He swallowed. "J–j–just . . . sssseeing how . . . you're . . . d–d–d–doing."

"Why?"

That threw him. "Uh . . . it's . . . m–my . . . job."

Her unblinking eyes assessed his for a moment before quickly turning away. "I didn't feel much like picnicking."

"O . . . kay."

The mute, discomforting silence stood between them like a solid brick wall.

"Any . . . th–th–thing . . . you . . . need?" he asked, trying to ignore the feeling of total failure that was squeezing him from every side.

"I don't believe so."

He gave her a perfunctory nod and stepped off the stoop. Guess that about ended it then.

She shut the door.

Turning, he trekked back to where Carla stood waiting in the growing shadow of the tall pines.

"Social thing, isn't she?" Carla asked.

Jack threw her a sad sort of smile. "C–c–come on. L–let's . . . get . . . going. M–mosquitoes will . . . be . . . out ssssoon."

Any other comments were lost in the quiet, but Jack couldn't shake the awful feeling that he was missing something about that girl . . . they were all missing something.

Standing a good distance from the window pane, Carillon watched them walk away. Wondering why she'd never find her place in the world. And wondering why she should even care . . . especially since Evie's death rested on her shoulders.

She was where she should be. Alone.

Just as her sister had been at the end.

# Chapter 8

Carillon reread the entry she'd already read several times:

*What a shock to find such a haven.*

*I'd not even been looking for it. But there it sat. At the edge of the woods, its long, fertile fields wrapped around a quaint white house and barn.*

*Why hadn't I known that this place even existed? Do they have children who attend school? Is there a wife here whom I could befriend? It's so close — it would be a shame not to strike up some sort of friendship with the owners. I wonder who they are?*

*Such a lovely place. And it suddenly makes my solitude here seem a little less daunting. So near . . .*

Carillon lifted her eyes to watch her footing on the somewhat overgrown path trailing through the lush, deep woods.

It had been days now. Days since she'd

seen anyone, including Mr. Tate. She knew the visitors had already begun arriving at Yesteryear. But she'd yet to see any make their way to her schoolhouse.

There were only two possible reasons for this that she knew of.

Either they felt the school building wasn't ready. Or she, herself, wasn't ready.

Well, she'd surprise them when they came. Unaccountably, she'd delved into the historical materials with a fervor fueled by the personal documentation in Miss Whitcomb's journal. Were a group to come through, she was confident that she could walk them through a very typical school day in 1850. And part of her longed to do that. To prove to these people that she could succeed.

With her intense interest had come another benefit . . . one that had initially escaped her notice. Her thoughts of Evie had lessened.

Oh, she still had them. But when they surfaced, they weren't accompanied by that feeling of utter despair. The guilt was still there, though. So she tried to push thoughts of Evie out of her mind and refocus her attention on the musings of Madeline Whitcomb.

Musings . . . It was the latest of those musings that had Carillon traipsing through this dense forest, trying to find a little set of farm buildings that, in all probability, were no longer standing. Something spurred her on anyway.

Clutching the journal in one hand and brushing aside insistent branches with the other, she kept walking, her eyes peeled for any clearing that might be on the horizon.

When it seemed she'd been battling the shrubs and overhanging branches for too long and that perhaps the place no longer existed, she stopped and took a deep breath. Smoothing a wayward strand of hair that had escaped from the combs holding it back, she glanced once more at Madeline's description, then turned and did a full scan of the area around her.

She couldn't see anything beyond the brambles and trees.

Then something flashed in the corner of her vision.

Pivoting in its direction, she strained to see it again. Nothing.

She shifted her weight and leaned to one side.

There it was again. A faint flicker. Like the sunshine reflecting off an object.

She strode in that direction.

Amazingly, in just a few steps, she found herself face-to-face with a large open area. One that had been totally disguised by the dense overgrowth and the waist-high grasses covering the small meadow.

A short distance past the waving blades of grass and heads of wildflowers they stood. A small white house. A larger white barn. Each looking regal amid the wild beauty of the woods but also seeming pathetic and worn from the unforgiving elements of time and weather.

This was it. It had to be.

The journal temporarily forgotten, Carillon waded through the quiet rustling weeds, the birds the only accompaniment to the otherwise bright summer afternoon. When she'd come within fifty feet or so of the house, she stopped, hesitant.

Insistent curiosity propelled her feet closer until she was maybe fifteen or twenty feet from the front door.

The covered porch sagged at one corner, and several of the spindles lining the rail were missing. Only traces of its previous white clung in stubborn patches to the gray, weather-beaten wood. Several windows were broken or missing altogether. She cast a glance at the second-story panes and realized it had been the sun's reflection against the dirty glass that had caught her attention.

Suddenly she felt extremely ill at ease — as if she were peering into someone's home, someone's privacy, even though it was more than obvious that no one had lived here for quite some time.

She almost felt as though eyes were watching her. From somewhere . . .

Carillon slowly turned and glanced back at the barn. The only movement was the constant wave of the grass and the occasional swoop of a bird as it dove from the roof onto the summer breeze.

Hesitantly, she turned back toward the now imposing house.

Part of her ached with curiosity to perhaps just step up the front stairs and peek in the front door.

But a definite sense of foreboding held her back. A sense that she wasn't supposed to be here. Wasn't welcome.

And the longer she stayed, the stronger the feeling became. Until it became overpowering. Overwhelming. Smothering. Terrifying.

Taking breaths in little gasps, Carillon turned and began walking as fast as her feet would take her through the tangle of grassy stems. She looked back just once.

Then she ran.

★ ★ ★

The late afternoon sun sparked a relieved feeling in Jack. The day was done. He'd almost forgotten how much he looked forward to the end of a day here. True, he enjoyed the visitors. And working with and getting to know the staff. But there was something about completing chores at the end of the day that left him satisfied, tired — in a good way. He distinctly remembered the sensation from when his family had farmed. Granted, they got in from the barn a lot later than most people who worked a normal nine-to-five job, but with that came the distinct feeling of having really accomplished something.

He felt that here at Yesteryear — to a point. But it was never quite the same.

It was with that very feeling that he approached his small cabin, eagerly looking forward to a quiet supper and perhaps some time with a good book before falling into bed.

"Jack."

The voice startled him. He spun around to find Bob puffing his way up the path.

Jack smiled. But his face changed as Bob's expression became clear the closer he came.

Jack held open the door to his cabin and ushered his boss in silently. Whatever the problem, Jack wouldn't have to ask. Bob was never one for beating around the bush.

He took a moment to scrub up at the washbasin before taking a seat at the small table. Bob had already made himself as comfortable as his obviously troubled position allowed.

"Have you seen the DeVries girl lately?"

Jack's heart sunk a foot or two.

"No."

Bob nodded, looking pensive. "We'd thought about opening up the schoolhouse this next week as part of the tour."

Jack nodded. He'd been aware of that.

"We'll have to postpone that for awhile . . . if not indefinitely."

A painful jolt seared through Jack, though it wasn't unexpected. "W–why?"

An equally pained look covered Bob's round face. "There's more things come up missing from the Mitchell House."

Jack sighed and raked a hand through his hair. "Sh–sh–she's . . . not even . . . th–th–there . . . any . . . more."

The older man nodded. "I know. But she knows what's there." He paused and kneaded his brow. "And Betty reminded me that the day of the employee picnic, Miss DeVries declined coming. The house was empty for several hours."

Jack closed his eyes at the horrendous sound of it all. "W–weren't . . . there . . . o–o–others who . . . d–didn't . . . come?"

"Not very many. And the few who didn't were away from Yesteryear, busy with other engagements."

He released another long breath. He had to admit, it didn't sound good.

Bob leaned his weighty arms on the table. "Now, I'm not as gung-ho to jump all over this as Betty is, but I am concerned."

Jack nodded.

"Since you're the closest to her new post, I'd like you to just watch her for a few days. Okay? Keep tabs on what she does. Where she might go."

"F–f–from what . . . I–I've . . . sssseen . . . she . . . d–doesn't . . . go . . . out much."

He shrugged. "Just keep an eye out."

A nod of disturbed agreement was all Jack could muster.

"We've set up a few precautionary measures at the Mitchell place, just in case." Bob hesitated, as if carefully choosing his words. "Just in case whoever is doing this tries it again."

The two men sat in mute silence for a moment or two. Finally Bob scraped the legs of the chair across the wood plank floor, easing up in a tired, weary sort of way.

"Guess I'd better go."

Again, Jack could only nod. Part of him ached too much to do anything else.

He opened the door and followed the big fellow's frame out into the fast-turning twilight.

"Ssssee you . . . t–tomorrow . . . then."

Bob nodded and started down the path.

Halfway across the small yard, he turned back. "Jack?"

Jack inclined his chin in question.

"You don't think she did it. Do you?" It wasn't a question.

Throwing a look at his boots, Jack shuffled them slightly against the dusty planks of the porch. Then shook his head. "No. I . . . don't."

Bob cast his own gaze to the ground then. His broad shoulders heaved in a sigh. "I sure hope you're right."

Carillon had never intended to stand there that long. She'd never even intended to come to this place. But in her rush to flee from the unknown eeriness at the abandoned homestead, she'd found herself smack dab behind Jack Tate's little cabin.

She could see the light from the lantern flickering in his window, and sheer curiosity had made her keep her place. Just for a moment. Just to see what he might be doing.

But she'd never expected him to come out. And certainly not with Bob Feldman.

Stepping back behind the cover of a nearby oak, she flattened herself against the trunk and listened carefully, trying to hear over the growing chirp of the crickets.

No conversation came.

Frustrated, she leaned back around, trying to catch a glimpse of the two. From her vantage point, all she could see was Bob's large frame going down the path and Jack's thin one leaning against the post of his porch. Just from his stance, she could see he was troubled. And some undefined part of her knew that she was the reason.

She'd been about to flutter off into a host of miserable memories — wondering why she always seemed to have this effect on people — when Bob broke the evening's quiet.

"Jack?"

Startled, Carillon peered out from behind the trunk and sought out Jack's dejected form on the porch.

"You don't think she did it. Do you?"

In the awful silence following the question, she closed her eyes. She'd been right. This was about her. One more thing had happened. One more thing for which she would take the blame. Maybe she wouldn't have to worry about being here for long anyway. . . .

But it was the words that followed that startled her more than anything else.

"No. I . . . don't."

That was it. Plain and simple. Jack, in his quiet, yet confident manner, had just exonerated her. Part of her warmed in a way she'd never experienced before.

She glanced in Bob's direction. Waiting . . .

"I sure hope you're right." With that, he walked away, leaving Jack to stand alone in the growing darkness.

From behind Carillon, somewhere in the deep of the forest, it came. That sound. That horrible yipping and howling.

Fear skittered up her spine, paralyzing her. What on earth was she supposed to do now?

Jack remained motionless on the front porch for a few more endless minutes, seemingly oblivious to the horrid sounds echoing through the trees.

Torn between wanting to run for the safety of his cabin and the need to keep her identity hidden, she opted for the latter. How could she explain her presence? How could she make it look like it truly was — her stumbling upon his place — as opposed to her sitting in wait . . . spying.

No. She must stay put. No matter what it meant.

How many minutes ticked by, she didn't know. With some measure of relief, she heard what sounded like the howls growing more faint. And in between her bouts of fear came the intense curiosity. She watched as Jack continued to stand, looking out into the darkness. In the very direction she needed to run in order to get to her own teacherage.

Finally, before complete blackness had fallen over the woods, Jack turned and slipped through the door of the cabin, closing it slowly behind him.

Carillon shut her eyes tight, waiting for a second or two longer.

Then, with a strength fueled only by a stronger fear, she sprinted across the grass . . . hoping . . . praying that she'd make it home.

# Chapter 9

Tracking down Carillon DeVries proved to be more of a challenge than Jack anticipated. Not that she had disappeared . . . not by a long shot. Every time he unobtrusively strode by the teacherage and schoolhouse, she could be found. Sitting in the yard reading, walking around the empty classroom, shifting and rearranging miscellaneous items, or somewhere behind the door to her tiny home, the entry open to the winds of summer. But there were other times. Times when her absence was curious.

At first Jack had promptly headed for Liberty Town — Mitchell House to be precise — even though he still had that certainty in his heart that she was innocent of the accusations brought against her. But neither had she been there nor had anyone seen her.

The only one who seemed to have caught any glimpse of her was Lynette, the cook. And Jack couldn't help but notice that the woman seemed more than a little nervous discussing her.

For a split second, he wrestled with doubts — maybe Lynette had seen her take something. Maybe she was trying to protect her. But when it came to any specifics, the middle-aged blond couldn't be of much help. She'd only seen Miss DeVries "at a distance" lately. And she always seemed "in a hurry."

"Except the day of the picnic," Lynette remembered.

Jack eyed her carefully. "W–what . . . do . . . you m–m–mean?"

"Well," she continued, rubbing her tired eyes habitually, "I saw her around the house here that day."

Again, Jack felt a knot grow in the pit of his stomach. "W–w–where . . . ex . . . actly?"

Lynette cleared her throat. "She . . . She was . . ." She kneaded her creased brow. "She was coming out the back door."

"Are . . . you . . . certain?"

She nodded emphatically. But her weary face still looked troubled.

"All . . . r–r–right. Th–thanks, L–Lynette." He tried to give her a reassuring smile. It didn't work out very well. He started toward Bob's office at the main compound.

"What will happen to her?" Lynette's small voice came from behind him.

He turned back, his eyebrows knit in concern. "I . . . d–don't know. W–w–we're . . . not sure . . . sh–she t–t–took . . . anything."

"Do you have any other . . . suspects?" It seemed an awkward word to use, and her face showed her embarrassment.

He shook his head.

"Oh." She brushed a wisp of hair from her face. "Good luck."

With a nod, he continued toward Bob's office, wishing and hoping and praying that all the signs that were so clearly pointing to Carillon were somehow wrong.

Day three.

*What on earth am I doing here again?* Carillon asked herself. Settled in the grass, which now waved over her head from her seated position, she was at least a safe distance from it.

It.

*You idiot. It's a house, for crying out loud. It's not like it's alive.*

Her head knew it. Her skittery conscience told her something else.

Alternately she delved into Madeline's journal and kept watch over the house. Yet each day she settled a little nearer to it. A little nearer because Madeline's writings urged her to. Or at the very least, took away some of the fear and dread.

The months of 1853 unfolded like some sort of novel under Madeline Whitcomb's pen and ink. And with that unfolding came new discoveries. For Madeline and for Carillon.

*Well, I've met him,* the entry stated. *William Henrikson. He's the farmer. The occupant of the charming little place I stumbled upon. He happened to be out choring one time when I "happened" by. Quite embarrassing, I must admit. But he didn't seem put out or startled by my appearance.*

*He seemed a jovial enough fellow. Polite, at least. He has an attractive face (I'm ashamed to even admit I noticed, but it's something I've always taken note of — faces) in spite of the beard he's obviously growing out for the upcoming cold weather.*

*And he has very kind eyes.*

*I felt comfortable around him immediately.*

*Like any well-bred lady, I introduced myself as Miss Whitcomb, the new schoolteacher, and politely made mention that I didn't think I* had any students by the name of Henrikson in my class.

With a slightly reddish face, he assured me that, no, I wouldn't. He didn't have any children.

He smiled cordially, and I continued on like a complete ninny, I suppose. "Perhaps your wife is at home," I mentioned. "I'd like to invite her over for tea."

This time a smile crept across his face. Then he informed me that, no, he didn't have a wife, either.

Now it was my turn to blush maddeningly.

Unsure of what else to say, I'm sure I made a perfect fool of myself. I vaguely remember saying that it had been very nice to meet him and that perhaps I'd see him at one of the community functions.

I think he nodded and agreed in a quiet sort of way.

Then I left and berated myself all the way home for being such a forward goose. But then, how was I to know he lived there all by himself?

I just pray that the school board doesn't hear of my silly behavior. That would be one way to lose my post *quickly — cavorting with and seeking attention from area bachelors.*

Carillon had to chuckle at the description. How different life had been 150 years ago. Different . . . and simpler. In spite of the fact that the times and customs seemed archaic to her way of thinking, she again found herself drawn in. Knowing she shared a common thread with this woman — even for the short amount of time she was at the teacherage. It was easier to imagine it . . . to believe it truly happened when she was living right there. So with each page, Carillon found herself drawn into the story of Madeline and her attraction to and interest in the area farmer.

The months in the journal flew along. Christmas came and went with a lonesome Madeline lamenting her station. Bad snows made it impossible for her to return to her family's home out east for the holidays.

Some kind neighbors had graciously invited her to spend the day with them. So Madeline had carefully dug through her stash of scrap material and made each of the children in the family (in addition to their mother and father) some quaint homemade ornaments to hang on their Christmas tree.

She'd been more than a little embarrassed

when she'd arrived to find that they had no Christmas tree. Apparently it wasn't a tradition that had caught on yet. Or more likely, the farm schedule just didn't leave time for such frivolities.

But to her further horror, another guest had been invited to the family's get-together. Mr. William Henrikson.

Savoring each description of their encounters, Carillon couldn't help but compare her own encounters with men to this.

Oh, how they paled in comparison.

There'd been more than just a few, Tony being the most recent. She tried to remember back to when she'd met him. It had been at a party — somewhere.

Had she noticed his handsome face? Probably. Definitely his body.

Carillon reviewed Madeline's thoughts. Had she noticed his "kind eyes"?

That was a gimme. Not a chance. She'd seen things in Tony's eyes, but kindness wasn't top on the list. Try excitement. Desire. And more than a little danger.

Kind eyes . . .

The only person she'd ever known who'd had kind eyes was her sister.

"Evie," she whispered.

Closing her own eyes, Carillon let a dance of memories sway across her consciousness.

She could see Evie's sweet face that last night. Her impish little smile, so full of life. Hope. Love . . .

"I love you, Carillon."

She tucked the sheets tighter around Evie's little, skinny body and gave her the usual Eskimo kisses. "I love you, too, Ev. Now get to sleep."

"Is Tony still here?" she asked.

Carillon sighed. "Yes. Good night." She flicked on the nightlight and started for the door.

"I'm scared."

With a slump of her shoulders, she turned around. "What?" She trudged back to the six-year-old's bed. "You're never scared." She plopped down next to her and began running her fingers up and down her ribs. "You afraid the tickle monster is going to get you?"

Evie's shrieks of laughter cut the tension of the moment, her blond locks bobbing all over as she tried to squirm out of Carillon's reach. After a few moments, the tickling ceased, the laughter died down, and Carillon smiled down at Evie. "I'm going downstairs now. Good night."

"I'm scared for you," the small voice came.

Frowning, Carillon sought out the wide

blue eyes. "Why are you scared for me?"

"Because. I don't think Tony's good for you."

Stifling a smile, Carillon smoothed back a damp curl from the little girl's forehead. "You've been listening in on Mom and Dad's conversations, haven't you?"

She shrugged her slim shoulders.

"Don't worry about me or Tony," Carillon whispered. "We'll be fine." She gave the comforter one last pat and stood up.

"But he doesn't know Jesus."

Closing her eyes for a long moment, Carillon turned around and let out a long breath. "Honey, not everyone . . . 'knows' Jesus. Not everyone . . . needs to." She needed to be careful here. Her parents would kill her if she tried to undo all they'd plugged into Evie.

Her sister bolted upright. "Yes, they do!" she declared emphatically. "If they don't, they won't go to heaven when they die. They won't get to see Jesus. They won't be with everyone else who loves Him."

Rolling her eyes, Carillon, yet again, took a seat on the edge of the small bed. "Look, Angel. Sometimes there are people who aren't . . . going to . . . agree with that."

"Why?"

She swallowed and thought hard. "Because they have other things to think about, I guess."

The thin, blond brows knit together in worry. "Tony needs to know Jesus."

Carillon suppressed a smile. "Why?"

" 'Cause then you both could."

This brought a frown. "What makes you think that I know Jesus?"

The sweet little face scrunched up in concern. "He knows you."

"Who does?"

"Jesus."

"And how do you know that?"

"He told me."

"He told you."

"Mm hm. And then you could know Him forever. And I'd see you in heaven someday."

"Bug," she said softly, "you don't need to see me in heaven. You'll see me tomorrow. Right here."

Judging from the little girl's face, it was obvious Evie realized she wasn't having much of an impact on her older sister. The thought must have disturbed her greatly, because she started to cry — quietly.

"Oh come on, Ev." She wrapped her in a hug. "Don't cry."

"I can't help it. I want you to be in heaven, too. I want you to see Jesus, too."

Oh, this was frustrating. How was she supposed to cope with all this nonsense her parents had infected her sister with since they'd gotten "saved"? With a muted growl of frustration, she grabbed Evie's shoulders and held her away from herself. "Listen, Evie. You talk to Jesus, okay? If He wants me to know Him, tell Him to let me know. All right?"

The little girl sniffled and wiped her nose, nodding somewhat morosely.

There. Maybe that would settle this for now. She moved toward the door again.

"Carillon?"

This time she stayed at the door. "Yes?"

"I'd give anything for you to have Jesus in your heart."

"Okay, Doll." She tugged on the knob.

"I would. I'd even die . . . if I knew you'd meet Him and be in heaven with me later."

Carillon whirled around. "Shut up!" The words were out of her mouth before she could stop them. "Just shut your mouth, Evie! Don't you ever say anything like that again. Do you hear me?" She marched over to the twin bed and stared at her sister long and hard.

The little face before her showed no remorse or fear, however. Just the same sad insistence it had held before.

Rubbing her hands across her face, Carillon blew out a long, ragged breath. "I'm sorry, Hon. I didn't mean to snap at you."

Evie nodded.

"I just . . . don't want to hear you talking like that. Okay?"

Another sober nod.

"Good." She placed one last kiss on the silky, blond head. "Good night, Yvonne Laurel DeVries. I love you."

The little smile returned. "Good night, Carillon Brooke DeVries. I love you, too."

Satisfied, Carillon made it all the way to the door and actually into the hallway before she heard her sister's last words.

"And Jesus loves you, too."

The sharp taste of saltwater brought Carillon back to the present and the pain she could never escape. Tears fell unheeded to the leather-bound journal on her lap.

"Oh, Evie. What did you say to Him?" She sniffled as her voice got lost in the ensuing sobs. "What did you tell your Jesus?"

"Wait a minute," Bob clarified. He replaced the small reading glasses he'd discarded earlier and looked over the employee schedule sheets that Jack had brought along. "You're saying that there's a possibility that she might not have taken these things?"

Jack nodded. "I–I've . . . known . . . it all . . . al–long. B–b–but . . . I needed . . . p–proof."

"And you have it?"

"M–maybe."

The older man sat back in his chair, patiently waiting for the explanation.

Jack leaned forward and indicated the date of the picnic on the employee roster. "Th–these are . . . the p–p–people . . . who . . . came."

Bob nodded.

"These . . . didn't." He jabbed his finger to a short list of names, among them, Carillon DeVries.

"And?"

"W–where . . . w–were they?"

Bob frowned in concentration as he went down the list. "Ed and Linda were out of town at a family reunion."

Jack pointed to the next name.

"Kent was at his sister's wedding."

Next.

"Margo and Julie weren't here yet . . . still coming home from college."

Next.

"Lynette was out of town at her husband's folks."

Next.

"Miss DeVries . . ." Bob let the name hang in the air. "She was supposedly at her cabin."

Jack nodded.

Bob looked a trifle frustrated. "Jack, I'm not following you here. Everyone seems to have an alibi except your Miss DeVries."

*Your Miss DeVries?* The wording wasn't lost on Jack. Ignoring the strange feeling that accompanied the phrase, he moved his finger back up the list to Lynette Pierce.

"Lynette?" Bob asked skeptically.

"Sh–she ssssaid . . . she . . . ssssaw . . . Carillon . . . the day of . . . th–the picnic. C–c–coming out . . . of Mitchell . . . House. H–how . . . could . . . sh–she . . . if she . . . wasn't . . . here?"

Bob didn't look convinced or impressed. "Betty already told me this. She'd come back to pick up her check before leaving. Simple as that."

"Before . . . leaving," Jack reiterated. "T–to . . . go . . . to . . . ?"

"Her husband's folks." Bob actually looked like he was growing impatient.

And Jack could feel the steel growing in his conviction and in his backbone. "Didn't . . . her h–husband's f–f–folks . . . pass away. Last . . . year?"

A startling look of comprehension washed

across the older man's face. He glanced up at Jack with curiously raised brows. "Uh, Jack. Would you mind tracking down Mrs. Pierce? I'd like to speak to her."

Jack nodded and was out the door.

# Chapter 10

Lynette Pierce looked less than comfortable.

Betty Haskins looked mortified.

"Bob," Betty began, her face in a troubled pinch, "I certainly didn't come here to point accusations at longtime employees —"

Bob stayed her protest with an upraised hand.

"Nor did we. And we didn't meet to hurl accusations at anyone. Merely to find out the truth."

Mrs. Haskins sighed heavily and backed rigidly into her chair.

Lynette continued to rub her deeply circled eyes.

Jack tried to stay unobtrusively in the background. He knew he was already involved, but he was more than grateful that Bob was handling this. He watched in amazement as his boss's face took on a compassionate look as he turned toward Lynette.

"Are you feeling well, Lynette?"

She shot her head up abruptly, seeming

surprised at the question. A quick nod. "I guess so."

"I was curious," Bob continued, "how your trip went."

Lynette looked over at Mrs. Haskins, then at her hand sitting quietly in her lap. "My trip?"

"The day of the picnic," he reminded her. "You weren't able to attend."

"Oh. Right. Yes. Uh, the trip was fine."

Bob nodded and shuffled some papers around in front of him as if he were the most relaxed person in the world. "How are Ken's folks anyway?"

"Fine." She almost met his eyes.

He settled his ample frame back into his office chair, quiet for a moment.

Jack held his breath. The tension in the room was unbearable.

"Betty," Bob began, "I just thought of something. Could you head down to the stock room? I believe there were some donations dropped off the other day and I'd like you to take a look at them."

Mrs. Haskins's thin brows hiked at least an inch. "But I thought —"

"I'd really appreciate it if you could look them over now."

Her reed-slim figure rose from the chair and whisked out the door.

"Jack," Bob addressed him without even turning around. "Could you go and ask Darlene if the new stocks have arrived yet?"

Without a word, Jack strode from the office and shut the door silently behind him. As he trekked to the business offices, he continued reviewing Bob's handling of the situation. He wondered if he'd ever garner such finesse when it came to dealing with people.

He knew he could read them . . . that was a gift he'd long been able to utilize. But to take it further than that . . . Jack sighed. Serious doubts plagued his mind — fueled by the insistent memories.

By the time Jack had seen Darlene and been waylaid by several of the chattier members of the staff whom he seldom saw, a good forty-five minutes had passed. The door to Bob's office was shut tight. Subdued voices could barely be discerned from the hall.

Not eager to intrude on the meeting, Jack leaned against the wall and waited. And prayed. In his heart he knew there were hurting souls involved here, and he hated to jump to conclusions, but when the Lord pressed something on his spirit, how could he ignore it?

Several minutes later, the door creaked

open. The first one out was Betty Haskins. Her thin face looked more strained than usual. She didn't acknowledge Jack's presence as she whipped past.

Next came Lynette. Her eyes were puffy and red, her face blotchy from the tears that were still running down her cheeks. Bob was close behind her, assuming an almost fatherly role as he stayed near, but not too close.

Wiping her face with her fingers once more, Lynette paused before Jack and gave him a shaky smile.

He tried to return it. "You . . . all . . . right?"

She shrugged her shoulders and sniffed. "I have some things to work out."

Jack threw a glance at Bob. The older man's face remained unreadable.

"I'll be praying for you," Jack assured her.

Again, the wobbly smile. "I know you will." She ran another palm over her cheek. "Good-bye, Jack."

She started down the hall, Jack looking after her. Bob caught his attention with a nod of his head, indicating Jack should wait in his office.

Closing the door behind himself, he took a chair and waited, passing the time alternately thinking, praying, and wondering.

Several minutes later, Bob returned. He sat heavily into his chair, looking weary.

Jack didn't have to ask. He knew Bob would tell him in his way, in his time.

"I guess we should pay a visit to Miss DeVries," the older man finally said.

A wave of relief flowed over Jack. He raised a silent prayer of thanks.

Bob rubbed his tired eyes and then leaned his arms against the desk. "How did you know? How do you always know?"

It was a rhetorical question. Jack only returned his gaze and waited for the explanation.

"It seems that when Lynette's husband, Ken, lost his parents, they gave him and Lynette a modest inheritance. Nothing grand, but enough where they could have paid off a few things. Unfortunately, and unbeknownst to Lynette, Ken had already picked up an unhealthy liking for gambling."

Jack winced, sensing where this was heading.

"Yeah. Seems he thought the little chunk would grow if put on the right numbers at the casino. Obviously . . . it didn't. It left him farther in the hole than before. According to Lynette, she started getting telephone calls from creditors wondering where their payments were. She thought Ken had been paying the bills."

Jack nodded, understanding. "S–s–so . . . the . . . antiques . . . were a . . . way t–to . . . make . . . m–money."

Bob shook his head. "You know how awful it is to find out something like this?"

Jack could only agree by acknowledging the growing lump in his stomach.

"Betty was absolutely mortified. She didn't know what to say. I did ask her to issue an apology to Miss DeVries, though."

Bringing a hand to the back of his neck, Jack rubbed it habitually. "W–w–what do . . . we . . . do about . . . Miss . . . DeVries?"

The older man steepled his index fingers to his chin pensively. "I think she ought to stay where she is. There's still the issue of her inability to deal with the public."

Jack shrugged. "M–maybe she's . . . c–c–calmed . . . down ssssome."

"I'll leave that to your discretion." The large man rose from his chair.

Jack followed suit, turning to leave.

"Jack."

He turned and met Bob's earnest eyes.

"Thank you." He reached out a huge hand.

Jack took it and warmed under the profound simplicity of the gesture.

"You're a good man, Jack Tate."

The words rang in his ears all the way through Liberty Town and on his trek toward the little schoolhouse. Was he? Was he truly a "good man"? And what did that mean?

When he compared himself to Christ, the only man he could think of whom he wanted to emulate, he knew he fell far, far short.

Yet when the obvious comparisons came between him and his brother . . . his father —

Jack halted that train of thought. *You don't need to go there. Don't even start.*

Before his mind could continue on the painful path, he found himself in front of the teacherage door. A whole new host of fears and inadequacies stared him down, disguising themselves among the innocent chipped paint and battered wood.

Shoving those doubts aside, he raised his fist and rapped his knuckles smartly against the panel.

No more than a few seconds passed before it opened. He stood face-to-face with the questions and curiosity in Carillon DeVries's deep blue eyes, only deepening his own insecurities.

Yet somehow, the trepidation evident in

those azure depths strengthened his resolve. His purpose. His mission.

Taking a deep breath and simultaneously lifting a prayer, he found himself offering her a smile. The first one he could remember ever attempting.

And what was weirder . . . she returned it.

He lost himself for that eternal moment, just enjoying the subtle complexities of this woman before him.

Before too long, he regained his senses and had the wherewithal to refocus himself on the reason for his visit.

Suddenly remembering his hat, he removed the thing from his head and instinctively raked his fingers through his hair. "G–g–good . . . morning."

Carillon tilted her head, the faintest traces of the smile lingering at the corners of her full lips. "Afternoon," she corrected.

He smiled again and tossed a quick glance at the toes of his boots.

"I–I've come . . . for . . . a . . . rrr–reason."

Her eyes widened slightly in anticipation, but her manner indicated no anxiety. No hurriedness.

He appreciated it.

Licking his lips, he delved in. "I'm ssssent . . . t–to offer an . . . a–pology."

The stare widened more.

"F–f–from . . . all . . . of us." He nodded in hopes that she'd get his meaning.

Tucking a thumbnail between her teeth, she looked uncertain. "You've found out something then?"

He nodded. "Th–th–they know . . . now. Th–that . . . you d–didn't . . . do . . . it."

She gave a slight nod. But her expression changed little.

Jack wasn't sure what he had expected. It certainly hadn't been silence. He shifted his weight and passed his poor crumpled hat from one hand to the other, wondering what on earth to do next.

"Well, then." She finally broke the uncomfortable silence. "Thank you."

He inclined his head and habitually replaced the brown felt hat.

Well . . . that must be it. Chewing at one corner of his lip and turning around, he started down the worn pathway.

"Jack."

The tenderness in her voice did more to halt his steps than any other tone could have possibly hoped to accomplish.

Slowly, he turned, waiting.

Her fair complexion seemed to be reddening suddenly. "I just wanted to say . . . thank you."

He nodded again.

Her slim shoulders heaved up and down. "Not just for . . . this. But for believing in me. No one's ever really bothered to do that before."

"Believe . . . in y–you?"

Carillon shook her head. "That you did means a lot. Well . . . thank you."

A quiet smile played with his lips. "You're . . . welcome."

"Wait," she threw out suddenly, as if she were afraid he might quickly leave. "I have something else to say."

He turned toward her fully and tilted back the brim of his hat.

This time she rubbed her slender fingers across her frowning forehead. "I want to apologize."

A little lump rose in Jack's throat.

"I'm sorry that I . . . made fun of you. I don't know what was wrong with me."

Jack took a deep breath and looked at the ground. Again, he found himself nodding. "It's . . . all . . . right. I–it's hhh–happened . . . before." He tried to give her an understanding smile.

Quiet warmth crept into her eyes. "It shouldn't."

A new and different warmth crept across Jack. One that felt good. Hopeful. Promising.

And with it came a new sensation. A new direction. And now, now that some of those barriers were gone, it was a lot easier to act upon it. "D–do . . . you — W–w–would you . . . have . . . t–time for . . . a . . . walk?"

She looked at him curiously. "A walk?"

"Y–yes. I–I'd . . . like t–to . . . show you . . . ssssomething."

Those intense, deep-set eyes studied him for more than a few seconds. In his heart he knew that she was asking herself if she could trust him, believe him.

He returned the unspoken questions with a confident eye and reached out a hand toward her. "Come . . . w–with . . . me?"

She hesitated for the briefest of moments, then stepped down from the threshold. "Okay."

# Chapter 11

Where Carillon expected Jack to take her, she didn't know. She honestly didn't really care. For some strange reason, she just wanted to be with him. Near him. He was the first person in a long, long time to have made an effort to befriend her, in spite of her hostility. Why? She needed to know. There couldn't be anything in it for him personally, could there?

He kept ahead of her, only by a few feet, periodically turning around to see if she was still following. Each time he gave her a smile that she'd come to recognize as only his. Shy. One side of his small mouth curled up hesitantly as if asking permission to be friendly.

When he turned back toward the path, she took the moments she could steal without his observation to study the rest of him. Maybe five or six inches taller than she, he wasn't any giant, that was sure. And in spite of his slight weight, he was strong. She'd seen him as he'd been working around the schoolhouse. What he lacked in brawn, he seemed to make up for with sheer determination and grit.

His light brown hair, normally stuffed beneath that hat, was cropped short, leaving the crown to spike up in a way that stood in sharp contrast to his mild personality.

He suddenly turned around again, leaving Carillon to hide a blush at a perusal she couldn't deny. She tossed her glance to the side of the path, trying to ignore the odd sensation racing through her heart.

But she didn't have to concentrate on her discomfort for long. Within a matter of seconds, she regained her bearings and realized exactly where they were.

Her head shot up and she tried to peer over his shoulder. They couldn't be headed to —

No. It was impossible. Why on earth would he be going there?

Yet that was exactly where they ended up — the same farm she'd been courting for the last week. The house seemed more "quiet" today. Less troubled.

Or did it?

She stared at the dark windows that made the empty eyes of the house. For how long, she wasn't sure. Before long, she felt him staring at her.

Rubbing her fingers across her forehead, she squinted in the afternoon sunshine and dared a glance in his direction. His golden brown eyes were indeed studying her. Waiting. Watching.

"What is this place?" she finally asked. It was a question she'd long wanted to ask, but there'd been no one to field it. Carillon knew what it once had been — Madeline had detailed all of that in her journal.

But what had happened to turn it into this?

Jack's broodish brow wrinkled as he turned toward the building. "Th–this . . . is . . . home."

His voice was so quiet she thought she'd not heard him correctly. But a small catch in her heart made her maintain her silence, waiting.

He tilted his head as he regarded the dilapidated structure. "Home." That time he wasn't talking to her.

Nor did he seem to remember her presence.

She watched as his boots carried him through the waist-high grasses, bringing him closer to the sagging front porch. He didn't slow, instead continuing up the half-rotted steps onto the faded boards of the decking.

"Jack." Her plea was none too confident, and it got lost in the wind that pulled and teased at her hair.

The front door creaked open under his grasp, and she watched as he disappeared into the darkness of the building's interior.

"Jack." She was more insistent this time. Her feet propelled her after him. Not for concern about him, but for herself. She didn't want to be left alone. Several quick steps got her to the porch, and she had to take several deep breaths before drawing the courage to actually follow his lead.

Steeling that resolve, Carillon yanked open the screen door and entered the dimly lit kitchen. The darkened maple cupboards, stained laminate counters, and faded linoleum seemed out of place in the emptiness of it all. There were no appliances. No furnishings. No decorations to make the house a home.

Had she expected there to be? It was vacant after all. But what about the feelings she'd had while being near it before?

A sinister chill tried to wrap itself around her, and she shivered in its wake. "Jack?" Her voice seemed little more than a whisper.

A creak from above made her jump.

"I–I'm . . . up . . . here." His tone sounded

quiet, yet assuring.

Releasing a breath of relief, she rounded a corner, grimacing as she brushed aside the host of cobwebs framing the doorway into what had obviously been a living room. The center of the wood plank floor wasn't darkened like the outer edges, a sign of whatever rug had warmed the floors in years gone by.

"Here." Jack's voice floated down from her side.

She turned and gazed up a narrow, steep flight of stairs. His open, fresh face was at the top of the landing. He beckoned her with a hand.

She eyed the painted steps hesitantly. "Is it safe?"

He nodded and descended a few of them, as if to allay her concerns.

Again, squashing her growing fears, she carefully placed one toe at a time on the treads, making her way toward him. He waited patiently for her at the top, but it was evident that his mind was elsewhere. He kept looking down the hall — obviously at one of the several open doors flanking the sides of the constricted passage.

Reaching the second floor, Carillon stifled a sneeze as the dust flew up in little clouds under her feet. Amid the dust, scattered bird droppings and other remainders of small rodents and animals littered the darkly stained wooden planks.

She quickened her pace when Jack disappeared into the room at the farthest end of the hall. Continually brushing aside the spider webs, she tentatively stepped into the small, dormered room, which barely appeared big enough to hold a bed, much less anything else.

More interesting to her was watching Jack.

He walked the small perimeter of the space, touched a series of nail holes in the plaster, and spent more than a few minutes simply standing at the broken window, his thoughts somewhere out in the wild fields beyond.

Carillon stepped back against a wall, leaned against the rough, cracking plaster, and waited.

"I . . . hhh–haven't b–b–been . . . here . . . in . . . t–ten years." He almost sounded remorseful.

Feeling prompted to say something — anything — Carillon found her voice. "Was this your room?"

Almost seeming startled at her question — or perhaps her intrusion into his thoughts — he released a deep breath and turned toward her. "No. Mmm–my . . . b–brother's."

She nodded. "What's his name?"

His intense eyes covered hers. "Jon."

Then he looked away again. Back to the out-of-doors.

"Small," she remarked, eyeing the limited space again. "Is he your younger brother?"

He shook his head. "Older."

Beginning to feel uncomfortable, with not much else to say or ask, she raised her eyebrows and slowly turned, taking in the nuances of the empty room. In one corner, a small door, evidently an added closet, piqued her interest. She started toward it and reached for the tarnished brass knob.

"Don't!"

The sudden strength of his voice made her jump. Instinctively, she took a step back as he crossed the floor.

Within the seriousness marking his features, she saw a sudden added softness. "I d–didn't mmm–mean . . . t–to startle . . . you." He dipped his head in apology. "Just . . . let . . . mmm–me." He indicated the knob with a tilt of his head.

Carillon retreated another step and watched with renewed interest as he tentatively gripped the handle. Curious. He almost seemed to hesitate, just for the briefest of seconds. Then, as if anticipating some wild occupant, he flung the door wide

140

open, taking a step back as it thumped haphazardly against the blank wall behind it.

Empty.

Save the dust and dirt that accumulate in time's vacancy.

Shifting her attention to Jack, she watched as he yet again seemed transported to another time, another place. His normally kind, albeit intense, eyes narrowed. And his hand found its way to the back of his neck, unconsciously rubbing up and down through his sandy brown hair.

Then, as quick as he'd been to target this room upon their arrival, he seemed just as eager to leave it. Carefully and deliberately, he pushed the closet door back into the closed position, letting his hand rest on the knob as the latch clicked in the eerie silence of the room. "Are . . . you . . . rrr–ready t–to . . . go . . . then?" He plopped his hat back on his head and didn't wait for her answer.

She followed him back down the hall, daring a quick glimpse into each room they passed, wishing one of them would hold some answers. They held nothing. Nothing for her, anyway.

In less than a minute, they were back outside, their backs to the proud structure as they strode toward the woods ahead. Carillon found herself almost having to run to keep up with Jack's surprisingly long, fast strides.

"Jack." She tried to catch her breath as she stumbled through the tangling grasses at her feet.

Just short of the woods' edge, he stopped, turned, and looked back at her. The apologetic half-smile returned. "Sss–sorry."

But he offered no further comment. While he slowed for her to keep stride with him, the words between them were lost elsewhere. And in truth, she didn't feel much like breaking the silence. She knew too well the necessity of silence. Ofttimes there were no words that could take away the pain, and it was more than obvious that there was pain associated with that house. She'd seen it written on Jack's face.

Never one to wish anguish on anyone, Carillon somehow felt justified, or at least vindicated. There was a certain relief in knowing that someone like Jack Tate, who seemingly had "everything all together," might have issues in his past to deal with as well. But what were they?

They'd reached the corner of the open area where Jack's cabin stood. The same corner in which she'd found herself on that night, hiding behind the tree, listening to a near-perfect stranger stand up for her. She warmed under the memory as she studied Jack again, glad that this time she could be nearer to him.

As if he abruptly realized where he was, he turned toward her and nodded toward his porch. "D–do . . . you like . . . coffee?"

She nodded and followed him up to the quaint porch, flanked with two homemade rockers. Shyly taking a seat in one, she unobtrusively tried to sneak a peek into the little cabin. She couldn't see much more than the roughly hewn table and chairs. In the background she could hear him puttering around with cups and the coffeepot.

By the time he returned with the warm beverages, the sun was just beginning to sink behind the overwhelming stand of trees on the western edge of the lot. As the sky darkened, the cooler evening air took its cue and began instilling a nip in the faint breeze.

She took the mug gratefully, letting the warmth seep through her fingers and hands, willing some of it into her bare arms.

Jack placed his own mug near the opposite rocker before disappearing into the cabin once more. He came back several moments later with a fuzzy, striped blanket, which he unfolded and somewhat awkwardly draped around her shoulders.

Noting the charming reddening of his

ears, Carillon felt the warmth she'd been wanting in her arms rising to her face instead. "Thank you." She tugged the edges around her and settled back against the comfortable chair. "You seem to come to my rescue quite often."

He let out a quiet breath of amusement as he shrugged his shoulders and eased into the other rocker.

The night birds were their conversation for a time as each sipped their coffee and occasionally stole glances at the other.

Jack drained the last of his beverage and set the cup on the floor. "M–may I . . . ask . . . y–y–you . . . ssssomething?" He leaned his forearms on his knees.

Carillon tucked her feet up on the chair, wrapping the expansive blanket around her legs as well. "I guess."

With a shy grin, he threw his gaze at the floor. "Where . . . d–did you . . . get . . . your . . . name?"

"From my parents."

He shot her a "touché" look and let out a quiet laugh. The first she'd ever heard. Subtle and masculine all at the same time.

She liked it. And she liked that she'd made him do it.

"Well," she continued, "it's kind of a weird story."

He eased back and waited, his face expectant and interested.

"My parents were somewhat a part of the leftover 'hippie' generation. They were actually a little behind the times." She smiled. "I think they wished they'd been old enough to participate more in the sixties thing.

"Anyway, they spent a year over in France, just knocking around, getting odd jobs here and there, walking wherever they might end up. At one point they were staying around the area of Provence, camping in some farmer's field, and off in the distance was this bell tower. . . ." She stopped as she watched his face. A most unusual smile was creeping across it. "What?"

He shook his head. "N–nothing. Go . . . on."

She shrugged. "You can probably guess the rest. They heard these bells tolling, I happened to be conceived while they were there, and voilà — my name was suddenly Carillon." She took a sip of her coffee. "Pretty weird, huh?"

"No. I . . . like it."

She looked at him askance. "You do? Why?"

"It's . . . d–different."

"Well, you've got that right. Anything else might have been better. Amy. Megan.

Jill. And it's not like I can go by my middle name . . . Brooke isn't much better."

She was rewarded with his light laughter again.

"Well, I've spilled mine. What's your name?"

He raised his brows, surprised. "Jack."

"Just Jack?"

Half smile. "Jack . . . W–William . . . Tate."

"Jack William."

He nodded.

Then she went out on a limb. "Jack and Jon."

His head snapped up.

"Do you have any other brothers or sisters?"

Slowly, he shook his head no.

"Is Jon nearby?"

Again, no.

With each little question, Carillon watched his face grow a little more miserable, his frame sink a fraction or two more. She stopped, suddenly wishing she'd kept her questions to herself. How would she feel if he were to press her about Evie?

"W–would . . . you . . . l–like t–t–to . . . hear . . . mmm–my story?"

She sought his face, and for some odd reason the misery she'd seen only moments

146

ago was gone. He looked serious and perhaps a little melancholy, but at the same time, he was peaceful.

"I don't want to hear anything that you're uncomfortable —"

He shook his head. "It's . . . all . . . right. I fff–feel . . . like . . . I–I'm supposed . . . t–to share . . . this."

"Why?"

His shoulders heaved up and down. "I . . . d–don't know." Those brown eyes pierced hers once more. "Mmm–maybe . . . you'll . . . know . . . why."

# Chapter 12

Jack closed his eyes, prayed silently, and hesitated for the briefest of seconds. Was he doing the right thing here? Was there truly a good reason for him to share this? But with each doubt came the internal affirmation. *Go ahead. Tell her.*

He settled back into the chair and tried not to let the intimidation take over. "My b–b–brother . . . Jon," he started, "is fff–four . . . years older . . . th–than I. And in about . . . every . . . w–way possible . . . w–w–we're totally . . . d–different.

"He . . . liked ssssports — I liked . . . reading. He . . . hated . . . the fff–farm — I . . . loved it. He's over . . . ssssix feet . . . t–tall — I'm . . . n–not." He tried to offer an ironic smile to lighten the mood, then shifted slightly in his rocker. "He had . . . n–no time . . . for God." A long gaze was sent in Carillon's direction. "I w–wanted . . . nothing . . . but Him."

That last pronouncement brought an uncomfortable silence as she stared into the depths of her coffee cup. So here was where it began. This was where he began to strike nerves.

And for some stupid and bizarre reason, Jack panicked. All the stories he'd been going to tell, all the fears and hurts he'd been somewhat ready to share — they all flew straight out into the cold night sky. Because he'd let his own fear take control again.

After several moments, Carillon broke the awful quiet. "So he was not kind to you — Jon."

Jack shook his head. If this girl only knew . . .

"Where is he now?"

A hard lump rose in his throat. "He's . . . he's . . . a fff–few . . . hours . . . from here."

"And you never see him?"

Another shake of the head.

"That's kind of . . . sad."

Inwardly, he had to agree. But how could he explain it otherwise? Especially when it had been Jack himself who'd made sure that their visits were virtually nonexistent. Jon hated him. He made no effort to conceal that fact. In spite of Jack's knowledge that he'd done the right thing, there would always be a part of him that grieved. Grieved over the fact that he'd lost his brother.

"Are your parents nearby?" she asked.

"N—no. They're b—both . . . gone." The lump intensified.

"I'm sorry." She gingerly placed the mug on the floorboards and pulled the blanket around her more tightly. "I know how it is to . . . lose someone."

Jack thought back to what he'd read in her minuscule folder. According to it, both parents were still alive. But what about — what about that sister? Before he could voice a question however, she spoke again.

"How long have you lived here?"

"Here?" He hiked a thumb at the cabin.

"Mm hm."

"Ab—bout . . . eight or . . . nine y—years."

"Almost since the time you left home then?"

He shot her a quick glance.

"Well, you said — back at that farm — it had been almost ten years since you'd been there."

Slowly, he nodded his head. "Right."

"What happened to it? The farm?"

He inclined his head in question.

"Was it sold?"

With a slight hesitation, he finally agreed. "Yes. It . . . was sold."

"Who owns it now?"

Now it was Jack's turn to begin to squirm.

Wasn't this line of questioning supposed to be directed from him to her? Suddenly he was finding himself being backed into a corner. "Yesteryear . . . owns it," he admitted, taking the last slurp of the now nearly cold coffee. "But wh–what . . . about y–you? Where . . . d–do you . . . live?"

Carillon looked thoughtful for a moment, then smiled. "The teacherage."

He smiled back and set his own mug down.

"My parents live in a suburb of Minneapolis. Edina."

"Heard . . . of it. D–d–does . . . your ssssister . . . live there . . . too?"

The previous stillness was nothing compared to the frigid reaction that his question received.

Carillon took a deep breath and abruptly stood. "I like your cabin, Jack. It's very . . . cozy." She peeled the blanket from her shoulders, carefully and deliberately folded it, and placed it over the rocker. "But I should head back."

Jack floundered to his feet, taken aback at her sudden urgency to leave. *Dumb, dumb,* he berated himself. *Way to push too far, Jack.* Would he ever learn to do it right?

She'd already started for the steps when she froze suddenly.

Studying her carefully, he tried to discern what could have made her face blanch in visible fear. Then she did it again.

This time he figured it out.

Somewhere in the distance of the woods, he heard them. A sound so commonplace to him that he scarcely noticed anymore. Their high-pitched yips and howls pierced the summer evening as they called back and forth. "N–noisy tonight . . . aren't th–they?" He stepped next to her at the top of the stairs and shoved his hands in his pockets, listening.

Carillon nodded nervously.

"H–hard to b–believe . . . ssssuch a . . . small . . . animal can m–make . . . ssssuch a ruckus."

Her wary gaze sought his. "Small?"

"Sure. C–coyotes. No b–bigger . . . than a ssssmall . . . dog. Scared . . . of their sh–shadows, too. They . . . ssssee people . . . and rrr–run in . . . the o–o–other direction."

"Coyotes?" Her blue eyes were barely discernable in the near-blackness of the evening.

"W–wait a . . . second." He retreated into the cabin, lit one of his lanterns, and returned to the porch with it. "Y–you . . . ready then?"

"What . . . why?"

"I'll w–walk you . . . home."

"That's not necessary. I know the way."

"It's d–dark."

"I'm sure I can make it just fine."

He wasn't going to win this battle, Jack conceded to himself. "Here. T–take this." He handed her the lantern.

She appeared both grateful and uncomfortable. "Thank you." She began to step down carefully.

"Carillon." Her name jumped out of his mouth before he could stop it. What was he supposed to say now? He wasn't sure. But her leaving — like this. It just didn't feel right. Shuffling his feet self-consciously, he gave it his best shot. "I'm ssssorry . . . if I . . . said anything . . . th–that offended . . . you."

She studied him for a long moment, then shook her head. "You didn't offend me."

Partial relief. But the barrier still existed.

"Good night, Jack." She turned, holding the lantern up, its whitish flame casting swirling circles of light on the path in front of her. He watched until she was out of sight, the glow of the lantern disappearing in the thickness of the dark trees. And he turned and ambled into the cabin, feeling like more of a failure than ever before.

Carillon stared at the journal in front of

her. Her normal fascination with Madeline Whitcomb's postings kept getting lost . . . lost in the memory of the evening's events or, more truthfully, in the memory of the conversation.

Every time she tried to picture the farm as described in Madeline's diary, it instead became the place she'd seen today. The emptiness. The loneliness. The isolation. And the troubled look in Jack's eyes.

Compounded by the things he'd tried to share at his cabin. His life. At least a portion of it. That he had stopped well short of anything truly revealing had been very clear. But why?

She knew there was more. Much more. But it seemed as if Mr. Tate had walls erected as well.

It might have been a lead-in, or so she thought initially. Something to get her to talk about her own reasons for being at Yesteryear. To get her to talk about Evie. But as she watched him, as she listened to him stammer his way through his memories, she realized it was something else — something much, much greater.

Jack Tate had shared — or at least had tried to share — a piece of himself with her, and she had a feeling it was a piece that not many others had seen, a piece that he didn't let show often . . . if ever.

The thought warmed her. And scared her.

She relished the warmth.

And fought it.

The last time she'd felt that way, it had built toward a "need" for companionship. For someone to share with.

No, she didn't want that.

She didn't want to be vulnerable.

Carillon stared down at the journal and flipped it shut. Unlike Miss Whitcomb, she didn't desire to find that "heart to respond unto her own."

But what else could she call it when she saw portions of Jack opening up to her . . . and felt her own walls trembling slightly at the prospect of being torn down?

The accompanying Bible that had befriended the journal all these years still sat desolately on the ledge of the small table near her bed.

That there were secrets in it, Carillon did not doubt. That they were waiting for her, she did not doubt, either.

But that her fear of letting go was still too great — that she knew.

No, if God was somewhere behind all of her walls, He was going to have to stay there.

And if Jack Tate thought it was his job to

help tear them down . . . then, somehow, it was her job to keep him at a safe distance.

Jack cowered in the corner of the barn, hoping the bales of hay covered him. It was only a matter of time until Jon unearthed his hiding place. He always did.

Short, shallow breaths didn't do much to fill his lungs, and he felt himself getting a little light-headed.

Then he heard it.

The scuff of Jon's work boots on the hay. No other noise. Just the imminent peril.

The shuffling of those boots stopped — just above his head. He didn't have to look up. He already knew what was there. A face so full of hate and contempt that it hurt just to look at it.

Instead, he picked at the green leaves poking out from a nearby bale.

"You had to do it, didn't ya?" Jon snarled. "You just couldn't keep your big mouth shut."

Jack started to shake his head, but it was no use. Jon wouldn't listen to him. He never did.

"I had those magazines hidden. There's no way Mom could have found them." He jumped into the narrow opening between the bales, leaving him almost on top of Jack.

Grabbing Jack by the collar of his sweat-shirt, Jon yanked him to his feet until his steely eyes were boring directly into Jack's. "You stupid, little rat."

The stomach punch came swiftly.

Jack gasped for breath while he struggled to stay on his feet.

But Jon never let him drop. Each blow, each kick, every fist hit its mark, without a moment's hesitation between. The only thing between them now was the volley of Jon's wicked anger.

After a time, when Jon was breathing hard with his effort, he let him go.

Jack crumpled to the hay, gagging, coughing, and gasping. Every inch of his body screamed in pain. Every inch but his head and face. Jon had long since learned where to place hits to avoid notice by either parent.

As Jon clambered up and out of the hole, he turned around and glared down. "It won't be the last time if you don't learn to shut up." He followed up the threat with a string of profane adjectives.

And Jack sat trying to breathe . . . and trying not to cry.

Then he was somewhere else.

The hay became hard, cold wood. And the dimly lit barn became the pitch black stifling air of a space entirely too small for comfort.

He reached out, groping for the knob. Desperately trying to find the door.

"Jon?" he croaked out. The panic started to rise. "Jon, lll–let . . . m–m–me . . . out!"

Finally, the handle fell under his grasp. Wrenching on the frigid knob, he turned it with all his strength — only to find himself crawling into a dimly lit sanctuary.

Meager light diffused by the stained-glass windows cast a cranberry glow across the vacant church. Vacant — except for the solitary casket fronting the dais ahead of him. Clumsily scrambling to his knees, Jack habitually brushed off his jacket and pants and ran a hand over his hair.

Feeling as if someone had tied leaden weights to his feet, he lagged down the center aisle, trying to catch a glimpse of the casket's occupant. Too soon he saw. The dark hair, the fragile features. The unwelcome look of death on her face.

Grief stole the majority of his breath as he tripped continually closer. "M–m–mom."

By the time he reached her side, the church was no longer empty. From all around him came the shuffling, quiet noises of a congregation. The old wheezing organ pumped out a muted hymn while uncomfortable silence lingered over the place.

Jack turned and watched as all eyes focused on him. Some filled with compassion and concern. Some filled with grief of their own. And one particular set that would not face him.

Sensing the end of whatever this was, Jack stole down the aisle, trying to ignore the burning in his eyes, the ache in his heart. The hopelessness that was trying to pervade his soul.

The heavy wooden doors at the rear of the building creaked open under the weight of his push and he stepped into . . . the barn.

Panic returned, infused with an overwhelming feeling of inadequacy. He shifted into work mode and instantly sprinted for the nearest milker, which was squawking noisily under the cow. He'd just gotten the machine off when another one started its protest . . . then another . . . and another.

Whirling around in confusion, he saw every cow had a milker on. And there were at least a hundred cows — maybe more. Where had all of them come from?

All were bellowing to be fed. But where was the feed? A quick glance in the feed room showed nothing. No corn. No feed bags. Nothing.

"Jack!"

He shuddered as the voice thundered from somewhere outside.

The noise around him fled into the background; he watched his father storm through the barn's side entrance, a heavy concrete block of some sort in his arms. His steps were staggered, his eyes bloodshot and watery, his speech slurred.

Jack closed his eyes and willed the vision to go away.

"Jack!"

The man was closer now, lifting the huge stone in his massive arms, a volley of curses shooting from his mouth like poisonous arrows.

Jack caught a glimpse of the writing on the huge stone in the man's grip:

*Alice Marie Tate*
*1949–1989*
*Beloved wife and mother*

He stared at the tombstone, terror-stricken. "Dad!"

"Don't call me that, you lazy little . . ." More adjectives followed — Jack wincing with each one, but his eyes never left the engraved letters on the stone.

Until he saw it rising higher and higher.

He found his father's reddened, enraged

face once more and hit the cement floor of the barn's alley just before the thing smashed into pieces around him.

And he ran. Like he'd never run before. Wondering if this time he would ever come back . . .

He sat upright . . . gasping. Wheezing. All the pains hurting all over again. In the darkness of the night, he couldn't see where he was, he couldn't remember. Fumbling to his knees, he felt the hard wooden floor boards. Where was he?

The closet?

He groped for the door. It wasn't there.

His foot struck something. Something solid.

Crawling toward it, he ran his hands over the smoothness of a blanket. The rough edges of his cot.

Relief washed over him.

Inching toward the opposite end, Jack felt for the lantern and box of matches and lit the wick with somewhat shaky fingers. Growing, orange light flooded his sleeping loft. He flopped his head back on the edge of the rumpled bed and took several deep breaths. *Thank You, Jesus.* The silent words were said from more than habit when he realized how close he'd come to tumbling off the edge of his ten-foot loft to

161

the unforgiving floor below.

"Oh . . . Father," he whispered, his heart just beginning to slow from its adrenaline-fueled tempo. "W–when? When . . . w–will . . . it b–be . . . done?"

# Chapter 13

"You know the rules," Bob informed him with a grin. "Get yourself out of here today."

Jack tried to smile back.

"And happy birthday." His boss waved over his shoulder as he tromped back down the grassy path, which was fast turning yellowish as the end of summer stole the green of nature.

August 20.

A date he couldn't forget — for a lot of reasons. Never being able to forget one's own birthday was one thing. Compiled with the anniversary of losing one's family farm made it downright impossible.

Now Jack had another reminder for that date: Carillon DeVries. According to her folder, they shared the same birthday. Ironic. Because thus far, they'd shared little else.

He sighed as he pitched another forkful of hay down into the barn's manger below. What he'd do with this day, he had no idea. He'd run out of ideas long ago. Weeks —

no, months ago — when it seemed Miss DeVries's attentions toward him turned polite, downright professional, at best.

Granted, she was doing her job. Very well. The schoolhouse tour was proving to be one of the more popular stops among the tourists. Jack, himself, had even snuck in the back of the building several times during her intriguing discourse of an 1850s' schoolmarm. He wondered where she'd obtained so much in-depth information that went well beyond the topical notes she'd received from Yesteryear.

Once or twice she'd caught his eye. He'd mutely moved toward the door as if to leave. But each time something made him stay.

Even Bob couldn't deny that she was causing absolutely no more problems. But she did not make any sort of attempts at befriending any of the other workers, either. And any closeness Jack might have felt or even presumed to exist that last night they'd spoken seemed to be all but nonexistent.

That had been almost six weeks ago.

He couldn't figure it out.

Had he done something to offend her? Said something to offend her? Maybe the sharing of his memories had been a huge mistake. 'Course, he hadn't shared that much.

Whatever it was, the frustration on his part mounted continually. On more than one occasion, he'd found himself poring over her folder again and again — trying to find some vestige of what had brought Carillon DeVries here. What had made her so hard. And alternately, what at times had suddenly made her so soft.

She was a puzzle. An intriguing one at that.

And along with those frustrations were the other emotions he tried so hard to ignore. The feelings he'd long suppressed but was having a harder time continuing to do so.

Guilt often accompanied his frustrations because he ranked them among desires as opposed to much of anything else. True, he wanted nothing more than to see Carillon DeVries free from whatever it was that haunted her, but for what reason? So he might have her? He couldn't deny the thought had crossed his mind more than once.

So he prayed. He thought. He repented. He prayed some more.

He was stumped.

Whatever past experiences he might have had with boyhood crushes, they paled in comparison. There simply was something

165

about Carillon DeVries that made his senses take leave.

And he was not accustomed to that.

Where he tried to make God and His Word the center of his thoughts and mind, for some reason he found himself spending what he felt was too much time dwelling on this new visitor to Yesteryear.

Thoughts of her interrupted his praying, working, reading, everything. He couldn't enjoy the mental imagery, either. Not when he found it an intrusion.

Determined to keep such thoughts at bay, Jack decided to spend the majority of his day down at Sutter's Lake. Maybe take a book, hang out in the rowboat anchored along the grassy shoreline.

Something.

Anything to keep his twenty-sixth birthday from being a completely miserable experience. He'd just have to realign his thinking — remember where he had been and where God had taken him. And be grateful.

Carillon lifted her eyes from the journal. She'd been reading in it for the last several hours — engrossed in the unfolding drama of Madeline Whitcomb's growing relationship with the local farmer William

Henrikson. Her initial internal sneering at the antiquated protocol of the time quickly abated when she reminded herself that this was no dime-store novel. This was written under the hand of a real young woman. A lonely, yet brave, young woman. One whom Carillon recognized as having far more courage than she ever would have hoped to possess.

Courage.

Or what did Madeline call it?

Faith.

Having now lost count of the times she'd tentatively picked up the worn Bible, Carillon found herself flipping through it and trying to find the passages Miss Whitcomb had detailed in her personal entries. They seemed so applicable to the struggles and feelings that the schoolteacher had been battling. Was it possible that this ancient book had anything to say to Carillon?

Noting that Psalms seemed to be a favorite of the author, Carillon paged through the thin sheets until she found the recognizable heading and began reading the passages that had been underlined at random:

*The Lord is my light and my salvation; whom shall I fear? The Lord is the strength of my life; of whom shall I be afraid? . . .*

*Wait on the Lord: be of good courage, and He shall strengthen thine heart: wait, I say, on the Lord . . .*

*He shall not be afraid of evil tidings: his heart is fixed, trusting in the Lord . . .*

*The Lord is my strength and my shield; my heart trusted in Him, and I am helped: therefore my heart greatly rejoiceth; and with my song I will praise Him.*

Frowning in concentration and trying to understand . . . comprehend . . . Carillon closed the book and thought. How was it that Madeline could draw such strength from this book? How was it that these words could dissuade her doubts and fears?

She didn't understand.

With a heavy sigh, she placed the Bible back on the chair next to her bed and stared out the window. In spite of the fact that she had the day off, she'd thus far managed to stay cooped up in the teacherage. There wasn't any particular place she wanted to go.

Lie.

There wasn't any particular place where

she felt she could go.

Jack Tate's cabin ranked high on the list.

She knew she'd resolved to steer clear of it, of the abandoned farm, of all of it. But as the weeks passed, she found herself growing more restless, almost like some internal force was trying to make her go out. Seek out . . . something. But what? She was sure Jack might know the answer to those questions. But could she face him? That was another story all together.

While she debated, the warm rays of sunshine streamed through the glass panes, silently urging her to leave her self-made cell.

With a sigh, she plucked up Madeline's journal and walked out into the early afternoon breezes, debating which way to go. An urge sent her gaze toward a trail on which she'd not yet set foot. Not sure where it led but confident she could find her way back all right, Carillon gripped the little book in her hand and started down the leaf-canopied path.

It meandered and twisted its way through the lush green woods, flanked by smaller trees, assorted berry bushes, and the intermittent fallen log. By the time she reached its end, she was surprised to find a rather large pond taking up the majority of a meadow area. The sun glinted off the bluish-green water while the tender wind pushed little wavelets toward the grassy edges. All else was still, save the bobbing of a small dory anchored near the shore.

Carillon's initial response to the scene was favorable. It seemed quiet, quaint . . . almost out of a picture book.

Until the memories crashed in.

Water.

The last place she wanted to be.

Whirling around on one foot, she started back in the direction of the path. But somewhere in the distance, she heard the muffled voices of a group of people. Tourists.

Closing her eyes in frustration, she threw another look over her shoulder at the offensive body of water. Which one?

She didn't feel much like playing tourist guide today — and it was her day off. That it was her birthday as well, she tried not to dwell on. In truth, she really didn't care.

But to stay here? Next to this . . . place?

The voices grew somewhat louder as the group traversed an intersecting path nearby.

Letting loose a long breath of resolution, Carillon picked her way through the wavering grasses and plopped herself down several yards from the shoreline.

There. Not too close. But still plenty of room for privacy.

Letting the warm beams of sun splay across her shoulders, she flipped open Madeline's journal and tried to find where she'd left off.

Until the loud splash startled her.

Jumping in the wake of the sound, she peered around, trying to find its source.

Other than the ripples fanning out near the shore, she saw nothing.

Fear getting the best of her, she scrambled to her feet, wondering if perhaps a bear or some other equally dangerous animal had somehow caused the commotion.

Then she saw it. Closer toward the middle of the pond. Someone bobbing along at a leisurely stroke.

Her heart contracted.

Instinctively, she knew exactly who it was.

Before she could hide, his head flipped around, flinging a short spray of water from his wet hair as he suddenly faced her direction.

He stopped.

For several moments all they did was stare at one another.

Afraid he'd think she'd been spying on him, she nonchalantly raised her hand in an informal wave.

He nodded his head in return and began

swimming back in the direction from which he'd come.

Chewing on a thumbnail, Carillon watched as he expertly paddled toward that little boat she'd seen earlier. Unable to keep her eyes completely busy elsewhere, she couldn't help but notice his dripping form as he emerged from the water. Clad in swim trunks, she was surprised to see there was more to Jack Tate than she realized. Despite his small appearance, it was obvious that hidden underneath his chore clothes lay well-defined muscles. She'd seen his strength and felt it that night she'd been lost in the woods. Here was proof.

Feeling herself blush, she nearly had to stifle a smile. When was the last time she had blushed? Had she ever?

Picking at the binding of the old book, she kept her eyes down until she heard him approaching. Tentatively lifting her gaze, she saw that he'd thrown on a T-shirt and another pair of shorts atop his swimsuit.

"Good afternoon," she said quietly.

He nodded with that endearing half-smile of his. "And . . . you." He stopped within several feet of her and ran a hand through his sopping hair, casting another glance out over the water. "Feels . . . great. Y–you wanna . . . sssswim?"

She shook her head. "No. Thanks."

He hiked his thumbs into the front pockets of his cutoffs and assessed her.

She tried to ignore the disquiet that brought on.

"Haven't . . . sssseen you . . . in . . . awhile."

With a shrug, she forced her gaze back out over the water. "Been busy, I guess. Lots of people coming through now."

He nodded. "Yeah. I . . . n–noticed that." Her gave her a little smile. "Y–you're doing . . . a g–g–great . . . job."

"Thank you." Again the maddening blush tried to overtake her face.

As if suddenly remembering something, Jack swung around and then back. "Hey. You w–wanna . . . go . . . for a b–boat . . . ride?"

She shook her head adamantly. "No, thank you."

"Really?" He nodded toward the little conveyance. "It's no . . . c–cruise ship. But . . . it's k–k–kind of . . . fun."

"I really don't think —"

"C–come on," he urged with a charming grin. "F–for . . . your birthday."

She stopped short and stared at him.

His grin retreated into a quiet smile. "I . . . get to sssee . . . the records . . . on . . . everybody."

That inner urge was prompting her again. She was trying her level best to ignore it. "It doesn't look very big," she said, eyeing the boat skeptically.

"It's n–not an . . . ocean-going . . . vessel. B–but it . . . works . . . for here."

"Are you sure it's safe?"

He cocked his head and smiled again. "I've n–never lost . . . any p–passengers . . . yet."

"I don't know. . . ."

He reached out his hand.

Carillon stared at it. So strong and capable-looking. She lifted her eyes to his face. Once again she saw that peace in the depths of his golden eyes.

Fighting every cautionary urge she'd spent years to erect, she stretched out her hand and placed it in his.

It was warm. Solid. It felt right.

Without another word, he led her, hand-in-hand, to the shore.

# Chapter 14

Well, she'd managed to get into the boat without too much incident. She tried to ignore the fact that shortly it would be taking her out over the open water. She also tried to ignore the fact that her heart trip-hammered when Jack assisted her into the little rowboat. What was it about his touch — his mere presence — that unsettled her so? Unsettled her . . . and gave her a profound sense of safety. An odd dichotomy.

Whatever it was, she tried to get over the next hurdle — swallowing her fear as Jack pushed the craft out into the water, deftly manning the oars in smooth succession. For some odd reason, it wasn't as hard as she anticipated. From across the wind came the trill of the late summer songbirds. The wooden paddles slapped the water quietly as the boat streamed across the calm pond. All else was still. And Carillon was grateful. Quiet was what she needed right now.

Feeling herself relax in the caress of the sun, she actually dared to drop an arm over the side, letting her fingers trail in the surprisingly warm water.

"Feels good . . . d–doesn't it?"

She let her eyes find his and slowly nodded.

"You . . . sure? N–n–no . . . swimming?"

Immediately she shook her head. "No. I don't care much for . . . swimming."

He shrugged his shoulders and kept heaving against the oars.

For a long time they simply sat, basking in the stillness of the afternoon, both of them seemingly unsure of how to break the reverie or even if there was a good reason to. Occasionally a slight catch of an eye or a timid smile would interrupt the serenity.

After a time, Jack finally found his voice. "Your . . . tour," he started, "it's . . . r–really . . . impressive."

She smiled shyly and tipped her head in a thank-you.

"I'm . . . curious." He tugged on the oars one last time before tipping them up and resting them on the gunwales, letting the boat drift lazily on the subtle current. "W–where did . . . you get sssso . . . much . . . information?"

Carillon shifted a bit and swallowed. "What do you mean?"

"Well, we . . . had a sssschool . . . teacher

. . . before. Her t–talks weren't . . . nearly as . . . interesting." He grinned at the confession.

Biting back a smile of her own, Carillon shrugged. "Actually, I ran across a journal. It's helped a lot."

He nodded and proceeded to lean back against the bow of the little boat, propping his feet comfortably on the side. "Must be . . . quite a . . . read."

She agreed silently.

In the far corner of the pond, a small fish jumped, temporarily shattering the mirrorlike surface. Carillon looked over at Jack, who now had his head leaned back as well, his eyes closed against the glare of the sun, its rays picking up the golden highlights in his hair — casting shadows under his chiseled cheekbones and well-defined jaw. He almost looked sculpted. Perfect. Why had she not noticed it before? Not a drop-dead gorgeous face . . . but fine. Full of character.

But was it truly only the physical that exuded that character?

Carillon knew better.

She'd seen it. In his eyes. In his walk. In his words. In everything about him. Had he drawn strength from the Bible as Madeline Whitcomb had?

Or had his past experiences, whatever they entailed, made up that portion of him that defied definition?

The curiosity burned at her. Glancing at his resting form warily, she drew in a deep, silent breath. "Jack?"

He opened one eye, peering at her under the sun's brightness. "Yeah?"

Shifting her gaze to her hands, she fidgeted with them. "Where does your brother live?"

Both eyes opened.

"I mean, you said he lives a few hours from here, right?"

Jack's sneakered feet plopped into the bottom of the boat as he straightened back up, his face looking more sober. "Yes. He . . . lives a few . . . hours away. Th–that's . . . right."

"Where?" Amazed, and somewhat embarrassed, at her sudden boldness, Carillon watched him carefully.

Letting out a long sigh, Jack picked up the oars again and plopped them back into the water with an unrefined splash. He began tugging on them with renewed energy.

*Great,* she berated herself, *let's just alienate him right off the bat.*

"How . . . much time d–do . . . you have?" he suddenly asked.

The question startled her. "Um, all day, I guess." She tried to throw in a meager attempt at a smile.

He nodded and gave a halfhearted attempt back. "It m–m–might take . . . that long."

"All right," she replied quietly.

As Jack continued to pull against the wooden paddles, the story unfolded. "M–my brother . . . Jon, is in . . . prison."

She tried to quell the sharp intake of breath.

"He'll b–be there . . . fff–for a . . . long time." A profound look of sadness swept across his face.

"Why?"

Not even meeting her eyes, but losing his gaze somewhere out over the tall treetops lining the lake, he began again. "He . . . killed a . . . girl."

If she'd been shocked before, her heart positively froze now. "What?"

He nodded miserably before finally finding her face. "Over . . . t–ten years ago now."

"What — in some sort of accident?"

He shook his head. "No." His eyes narrowed as he scanned the horizon again. "He raped . . . her. Then sssstrangled her."

Carillon felt that iciness creep into her gut

as she looked down at the water, not knowing what to say — and wishing she'd not said anything.

"It sssstarted a . . . long time . . . b–before that. He'd . . . always k–kind of . . . been . . . in and out . . . of t–trouble." He kneaded his forehead as if trying to remember. "I d–don't know . . . what age he . . . sssstarted buying . . . the m–magazines." He shook his head. "It . . . w–went downhill . . . from there."

"How old was he . . . when it happened?"

"Nineteen."

"And the girl?"

"F–fifteen."

Nausea crept into her.

Two distinct pools formed in Jack's eyes. "Nice . . . girl, t–too."

"You knew her?" she whispered.

He nodded. "Sh–she was . . . our neighbor." Wiping at his eyes with his palms, he dropped the oars with a thunk back into the boat and raked his fingers through his hair. "By . . . the time th–they . . . found her b–body, I . . . knew." He rubbed at his jaw thoughtfully. "I . . . just knew."

"What happened then?"

"The t–trial. P–pretty short. D–didn't take them . . . long . . . to l–look at . . . the obvious . . . evidence."

Her heart constricting a fraction more, she studied him carefully. "And you had to testify, didn't you?"

"Yep." He cast his gaze back over the scenery. "I p–put my . . . own brother . . . in jail."

Without a moment's hesitation, Carillon carefully slid off her seat and moved one closer to him. "No, you didn't," she said. "No, you didn't."

He sought her face as she inched closer to him.

"His own actions put him there. What if you hadn't said anything? What if he'd gotten away with it? What might he have done later?"

Behind the golden depths, a moment of clarity resurfaced as he stared at her.

Carillon reached out and took one of his hands. "Jack, you did what was right. Responsible."

He remained silent.

For some unknown reason, she forged on. "There's more to this, isn't there? It doesn't end or begin with this whole ordeal — the trial?"

His full lips pursed momentarily. He shook his head.

"That closet upstairs in your house . . ."

The nod finished her sentence.

"And that was the least of it, wasn't it?" Suddenly, somehow, she knew. Her grip tightened on his. "You did the right thing," she repeated.

He kept staring at their clutched hands. "He's . . . still m–my . . . brother."

"Yes." She swallowed hard. "And you still love him — in spite of it all. Don't you?" It wasn't a question.

He took a deep breath. "I l–looked up . . . t–to him. Fff–for so . . . long."

"And now?"

He finally looked into her eyes. "I . . . found out — you c–can't . . . look to . . . men. Only . . . Jesus." He smiled somewhat shakily.

Carillon retreated a fraction at his pronouncement. Now she was totally at a loss as to what to say.

"Th–thank you," he said quietly.

"For what?"

"For . . . listening. And . . . understanding."

Slowly, she withdrew her hand. "For listening . . . ? Sure." She tried to smile, but failed miserably. "But don't ever blame yourself, Jack." A painful lump rose in her throat. "I know what it's like to be responsible for someone's — for someone. And to blow it. You are not one of those people."

Now it was Jack's turn to look confused. But if he held questions, he was gracious enough to silence them — for now. Carillon was eternally grateful.

Off on the skyline, a distant roll of thunder rumbled.

Both of them cast their eyes in that direction. A long ways off yet, but steadily moving in, a long, wide band of black clouds was eating up the blue sky.

Jack slowly pulled his fingers away from hers, and Carillon was surprised at the keen disappointment that flooded her soul. Plucking up the oars, he began heading back toward the shore. "G–guess we'd better . . . get in."

She nodded in agreement while her heart railed at the coming storm. For having started the day desiring to be totally alone, now she found herself wishing she could remain in Jack's company.

The quiet of the slapping paddles seemed a good interlude between their ride and the reality that lay awaiting them at shore. Carillon tried to sort out her feelings as they approached, finding it difficult to do so while in his presence. One question came into view.

"Jack?"

He raised his chin and waited.

"You —" She cleared her throat. "You read your Bible, right?"

He nodded without hesitation. "I'd never . . . have b–been able . . . to m–make it . . . without."

"Why?"

He looked at her curiously.

"I mean, what's in it? Well — I know what's in it . . . but what do you get out of it?"

His face softened. "Life. Strength. Hope . . . w–when all hope . . . is gone."

Carillon bit her lip as she contemplated his answer. "All just from those pages? Those words?"

This time he shook his head. "Not . . . the words. From the . . . author of . . . those words."

"God."

He nodded and smiled a little. "If I . . . sssstruggle at . . . t–times, all I . . . have t–to . . . do is . . . go back. B–back to . . . the beginning."

She nodded as if she understood. She didn't, though. *The author? God? How could Jack find Him in there?* She'd read Madeline's similar thoughts along those lines and had been just as confused.

Carillon had read the words, too. And

that's just what they were. Words on a page. Nothing more.

She started to ask one more question and then thought better of it. She didn't want to appear totally ignorant. So she merely nodded a thank-you for his answer and waited until they pulled up on shore, her head swimming in confusion and curiosity.

The darkening sky had as yet to spill any of its threatened rain, but it kept getting more sinister by the minute. Jack kept one eye heavenward as he jogged along the path cutting through the woods toward the compound. If his clock had been right, he still had time to make it there.

As his steps took him nearer, he reflected on the afternoon. What could have been a miserable, lonely day had surprised him. Doubly.

That Carillon had even approached him had been enough of a shock. That she'd agreed to spend some time with him had been a pleasurable bonus. Until the subject matter had grown serious.

But amazingly, God, in His goodness, had used that as well. Normally such reminiscence would have put Jack into a funk for days, but this time telling his story had been only a sweet release. An understanding heart had listened. He thanked God for that.

But alternately, he felt a tugging at his soul — an urgency about Carillon's own heart and his own feelings of inadequacy . . . whatever the reasoning behind them all. He thought this gesture, as small as it might be, would be appropriate.

With a confident stride, he entered the door of the gift shop, waving at the two young women behind the counter.

"Hi, Jack," they chorused in unison.

He smiled back and headed in their direction.

"Need something?" Karen, the younger of the two, asked.

"Yeah." He cleared his throat. "D–do you . . . have any . . . journals?"

"Like diary-type journals?"

He nodded.

"Sure. We have a really nice selection back here." She beckoned him to follow her to the rear of the store where a long shelf stood, filled with an assortment of bound books. She pulled off a few plain, leather-bound varieties for him to peruse. "Like these?"

He glanced at the offerings, then studied the shelf again, his gaze shifting toward a different one. A cream-colored fabric encased the volume, the center a showcase for a few delicate, pressed-and-dried wild-flowers lying behind a protective plastic window. He picked it off the ledge and smiled. "This . . . one. Please."

Karen inclined her head in deference to his choice. "Alrighty."

"And c–could you . . . wrap it for . . . me?"

She agreed and headed back up to the counter.

Jack followed her all the way, smiling.

# Chapter 15

Carillon settled back onto her small bed, re-reading Madeline's entry one more time:

> *It seems the more time I spend with Mr. Henrikson, the more he becomes "William" to me — though I'd never dream of calling him that to his face. In my heart, I already have. And unless I'm under completely false assumptions, I think he must feel something for me as well. But here we are — the guidelines for my occupation and good society requiring us to keep our distance.*
> *Frustrating.*
> *How can two hearts connect with all the barriers between?*

Carillon released a long breath and glanced out at the growing darkness of the impending stormy afternoon. How indeed?

Barriers? She had them. Jack had them.

But perhaps she, too, was being presumptuous. Had Jack really indicated that he'd shown more than a passing interest in her? Anything more than any other person at Yesteryear? Jack Tate was a caring person. He seemed to love everybody. And everyone loved him right back.

Love.

Carillon swallowed hard around the mere thought of the word. She couldn't let herself even close to that. She wouldn't. The last person she'd loved was gone. Evie was gone forever — and it was all Carillon's fault.

No, she wouldn't wish her love on anyone — assuming she could even muster the emotion anymore.

But as vainly as she tried to deny her feelings, every facet of Jack flooded her mind. Every movement, every compassionate glance, every touch. Each sweet, stammered word.

Frustration mounted that she'd allowed herself to become so soft. What had happened to her walls? To her fortress she'd erected so perfectly? Tony hadn't come close to it. Nor had any of the others. How could Jack, this person she'd known for such a short time, knock down such a vital protection with his first glance at her?

Her eyes trailed back to the diary:

*I know all sense of propriety is lost*

189

*when my mind succumbs to these fanciful notions. But I've simply never met anyone like William. All the dandies from the cities east do not hold a candle to him. Where they're fine and regal, he's strong and steadfast. Where they simper and complain, he frowns in concentration and is diligent. Where they blatantly feast their eyes upon a woman's beauty, he makes me feel one hundred times more beautiful simply by treating me like a lady — even though the times we've shared together are so few.*

Running a hand through her hair in amazement, Carillon couldn't stifle the smile. This man sounded so much like Jack.

*I pray that my thoughts and emotions won't supercede God's plans for me. But I'm reminded so much of Solomon's wisdom in trying to understand the complexities of this scenario:*

*"There be three things which are
too wonderful for me,
yea, four which I know not:*

*The way of an eagle in the air;
the way of a serpent upon a rock;
the way of a ship in the midst of
    the sea;
and the way of a man with a
    maid."
. . . the way of a man with a maid.*

*Father, You've created us to be this
way. To interact this way. To love this
way. Guide me in Your will.*

Carillon read the words again. How could
she not agree? The effect that Jack had on
her resisted any definition. Any understanding.

Her thoughts were broken by a strange
sensation. From her front door, a subtle
shuffling could be discerned. Then silence.

Remaining on her bed, she glanced out
the small side window but saw nothing. Curiosity getting the best of her, she rose and
crossed to the door, letting it creak open on
its rusty hinges.

The meadow before her was quiet, not
giving up any secrets. Perhaps it had just
been a small animal nosing around.

She started to shut the door, but then she
saw it.

A small parcel lying on the top step, propped against the threshold. Wrapped in a muted yellow paper, a simple length of lace gracing the front. And a little envelope taped alongside it.

A lump rose in her throat as she stared at the gift. No question who'd delivered it. With shaking hands, she bent down to retrieve the package and looked once more out across the waving grasses. Nothing.

Retreating into her cabin, she hesitantly detached the envelope and pulled out the card. A pen-and-ink sketch of an aged barn surrounded by tall wildflowers and prairie grasses graced the cover. Biting her lips, she eased the card open and slowly drank in the words written in Jack's hand. A deliberate, masculine scrawl that seemed . . . him:

*No one should have to celebrate a birthday alone. I'm glad you were here to share mine. And whether you wanted company on your own day or not, I'm equally glad I was the one to be with you.*

Her heart stalled for a moment at the pronouncement — then she warmed under its ardor.

*You mentioned the journal you'd been reading. Journals can be powerful tools in helping us understand ourselves — especially as we look back at all God has done for us and through us. I've kept one for a number of years. And hoping I'm not being too presumptuous, I thought you might be interested in one, too.*
*Happy Birthday, Carillon.*
*Jack*

Laying aside the card, she unceremoniously tore into the paper and pulled out the simple but elegant little book. And for an uncomfortable, emotional moment, her eyes filled with tears. Cracking it open, she saw her name written carefully on the inside cover. She was overwhelmed with the thoughtfulness, the generosity — and the memories. . . .

"Happy Birthday, Lon!" her little voice chirped in its normal four-year-old exuberance.

Carillon grinned and hugged Evie to her. "Thanks, Bug."

"I have something for you!"

"Oh, Honey, that's all right. You don't have to give me anything —"

"I want to. Wait here!" She sprinted

193

around the corner while Carillon smiled and returned to her bowl of breakfast cereal.

It wasn't two seconds before the little imp was back, her arms held awkwardly behind her back. In a fumbling of fingers and arms, she produced the very crudely wrapped gift, covered with probably more than twice the wrapping paper needed and three times that amount of tape.

Stifling a laugh, Carillon took the thing and proceeded to rip away at the inch-thick barrier of transparent adhesive. "What do we have here?" she asked, her eyebrows rising expectantly.

Evie just stood with her arms clasped behind her back, twisting back and forth in anxious anticipation, the grin covering her little face.

By the time Carillon reached the interior, a small fuzzy leg covered in black-and-white spots stuck out from the paper.

Immediately she knew what the gift was, and her fingers stalled as she looked at her little sister.

Evie jumped up and down. "Open it! Open it!"

Carillon finished peeling back the paper to reveal exactly what she'd guessed. A small Beanie Baby dalmatian — Evie's favorite. The one she had to have when going to bed, going on trips, even just to the grocery store. The little dog was never separated from her.

"Evie," she started, "this is —"

"Dean!" the little girl proclaimed gleefully.

Carillon smiled. "Dean" had been toddler Evie's attempts at saying "Beanie." "He's . . . great." She stared at her sister. "But I can't take Dean."

The face fell a fraction. "Why?"

"Well . . . he's your special dog. I wouldn't want him to get lonely without you."

A frown started across the little girl's face. "He won't be lonely. I know you'll take good care of him. And you'll love him as much as I do."

"Sure, Hon. But don't you think —"

"Lon, I want to give him to you. It's all I have to give you."

Carillon fought back a few tears as she grabbed Evie in a fierce embrace. "You don't have to get me anything, Bug. You are more than enough." She pulled back and ruffled the curly mop of hair. "But if you really want me to have Dean . . ."

"I do! I do!" The jumping began again.

"Okay." Carillon nestled the little dog next to her face and smiled. "But you'll have to promise to take care of him for me while I'm at school and stuff."

Evie nodded earnestly.

Carillon's heart swelled at the memory. Was there nothing that Evie wouldn't have done for her? Clutching Jack's gift, she stroked the smooth cover and frowned. So giving. There were more and more similarities that she saw between Evie and Jack all the time. Why?

Releasing a long breath, Carillon placed the book on the table. Well, she wasn't going to let this opportunity go by. She'd been nurturing her selfish side for most of her life . . . now it was time to learn some lessons from her little sister. To give back while she still could. Because she'd missed the chance once, she wouldn't let it happen again.

Heading back to the door, she peeked her head outside. No rain yet. Just the smell of it soon to come. Good enough. A little rain never hurt her. And she had a mission to accomplish.

Pulling the door shut behind her, she started in the direction of the compound. There had to be something she could find for him. Something that would show her appreciation.

Something that would make Evie proud of her.

★ ★ ★

Jack had a hard time containing his grin as he strode back to his cabin. He'd struggled with the option of handing her the gift himself or just leaving it. He opted for the latter — not wanting to push her. Intimidate her. It was better this way.

And it felt great.

By the time he reached his porch, he noticed something unusual. What? Stealing a glance around the barnyard, he noticed all was quiet. Too quiet. The guinea hens who normally fussed and cackled around the perimeter of the small farm were nowhere to be seen.

He trudged toward the small building that housed the chickens and poked his head in. No, they were all there. Sitting in their boxes, albeit nervously. Their uncomfortable shifting and turning not lost on him, Jack pulled his head back outside and noticed for the first time the complete stillness in the air.

The breeze that had played through the trees all afternoon had died away. No birds sang. Even the insects were silent. It was eerie.

Casting an eye at the sky, he felt his stomach roil up. The blackness was much nearer now. But worse was the sky fronting the inky clouds. It held a bizarre greenish glow — one that Jack remembered only a few times from his childhood.

Sprinting toward the cabin, he took the steps in one leap and stormed through the door. He dug the battery-powered weather radio from one of the cupboards and flicked the thing on. He was immediately greeted by the attention-grabbing monotone beeps of the weather alert system.

Waiting a few seconds more, he listened for the announcer's voice, the crackling of the airwaves distorting the words every so often. "A severe thunderstorm is moving in a wide band across the west-central portion of the state. Be alerted that this storm could contain heavy rains, hail, and damaging winds. If you're out of doors, seek shelter immediately."

The station crackled again, and Jack picked up the radio, fiddling with the antenna and shaking it impatiently.

From outside the still-open front door, Jack heard the wind pick up as the leaves on the trees began to rustle — first slowly, then more forcefully.

The radio voice returned.

"We have several reports of funnel clouds sighted along the border of Minnesota and Wisconsin — and more sightings east."

Outside, the wind intensified, whipping the tall pines ferociously, their slender trunks bowing down to the strength of the force moving in.

Jack ran to the door and looked at the sky. It was a churning, turbulent mixture of green and gray and black. It looked anything but good. Across the yard, one of the shed doors began banging haphazardly back and forth.

All Jack could think of was Carillon. Out in the middle of that open meadow — the teacherage hardly in any condition to withstand strong winds. Without a second thought, he dashed out, just as the first fat drops of rain began pelting the ground.

He had to get to her — get her to Liberty Town, where they'd be safe. Just until this thing blew over. He ran, the wind at his back propelling him along, the scent of something ominous hanging in its crest.

And in the now-vacant kitchen, the weather radio blared out its warning to no one. "Seek shelter immediately in a basement or sturdy interior room with no windows. Do not go outside."

# Chapter 16

While it looked at first like it might hold off for a time, instead the inclement weather barged onto the scene like the snapping of a whip. By the time Carillon reached Liberty Town, the wind was buffeting her so fiercely she could scarcely push her way through it. The wicked drops of water bombarded her like so many arrows. She was having a hard enough time just trying to catch her breath. Realizing she couldn't continue toward the compound, she stood in the middle of the main street, vainly peering against the sheets of water blurring her vision.

From somewhere under the howl of the wind, she heard a voice. Faintly.

"Carillon!"

Shielding her eyes against the torrential rain, she searched for the source of the voice.

"Carillon! Over here! The house!"

She turned and made out the form of Paul, the blacksmith, battling his way toward her. Never so grateful to see another human being, she didn't hesitate when he offered his hand and arm to help her across the yard toward the Mitchell House. As they walked, a section of the white picket fence uprooted and went cartwheeling in front of them. Paul shielded her with an arm and glanced around, looking for any more debris.

Finally, all but dragging her to the side door at the house's foundation, Paul helped her down the wet, slick stone steps and pushed through the heavy wooden door. While he grunted as he tried to slam the thing closed, Carillon's eyes adjusted to the dim light flickering in the center of the small, dank-smelling room. All the residents of Liberty Town were huddling against the far wall, blankets and other miscellaneous wraps scattered among them.

Carillon released a long breath, realizing that she'd probably been holding it since the wind had kicked up so suddenly. Paul had managed to latch the door and stood at her side, his hair plastered against his head, his white work shirt almost transparent with moisture.

"You okay?" he asked breathlessly.

She nodded and realized she, too, was soaking. Carla came over with a blanket and tossed it around her shoulders. Carillon accepted it gratefully, trying to wring some of the excess moisture from her hair. "Some storm."

The others looked at her soberly. A few nodded.

"When do you think it will blow over?" she asked.

Paul looked the most morose. "I don't know," he breathed, reaching for another blanket someone was handing him. "I don't like the looks of this one."

Before the words were completely out of his mouth, an excruciatingly loud *Pop!* thundered from outside. Everyone jumped in its aftermath.

"What was that?" one of the men asked.

He was answered by a load creaky groan, a dull thud, and the unmistakable shattering of glass.

"Come on," Paul urged Carillon and everyone else. "Let's back up against the far wall as much as we can."

Dumbly shuffling along with the others, Carillon looked over her shoulder and watched the plank door shudder on its heavy hinges, the invisible monster outside trying its best to break in.

Huddled with the others in a tightly knit clump, Carillon watched the anxious faces and suddenly wished that Jack were here.

She always felt better when Jack was nearby.

Jack!

Her arm shot out, grabbing Paul's shoulder. "What about Jack?"

A serious frown creased his brow, but he didn't hesitate in giving his answer. "Jack'll be fine. All the farms have root cellars. He'll know what to do."

"Are you sure?"

Paul nodded again in reassurance.

Before a remnant of peace could soothe her, she heard it. So did the others apparently. Their faces turned toward the door, their eyes wide . . . anxious.

From somewhere beyond, and moving steadily nearer, a distant hum . . . then a rumble.

"Oh, sweet Jesus . . . ," someone behind Carillon prayed.

The rumble fast grew into a roar, and had she not known better, Carillon would have guessed that they were immediately under a train track.

"All right, everybody," Paul said in an authoritative voice, "heads down. Cover up as much as possible!" The order turned into a yell as the clamor outside evolved into a deafening cacophony that defied comparison. All Carillon knew was that for as long as she lived, she never wanted to hear it again. "And pray!" Paul yelled again. "Pray hard!"

For the first time in her life, she had no problem with that. "Please, God," she whispered, her voice lost even to her own ears in the din. "Please be with Jack. Please . . ."

Jack couldn't see anymore.

He fought and struggled and gasped for breath in what suddenly seemed to be a vacuum.

He knew the teacherage was just ahead. Occasionally he'd catch a glimpse of the white frame before him. Then it would be eaten up again in the fury of the elements. Accumulating as much breath as he could, he shouted for all he was worth. "Carillon!"

Stupid. He couldn't even hear himself. How was she going to hear? No, he'd just have to get there and get her out.

From behind him, a snap and pop prompted his feet to propel him forward just as a medium-sized pine crashed to the ground. Then the roar approached, shaking the ground, the air, and the sky as it ate up all in its path.

Squinting against the dismal gray and into the yawning black beyond, Jack's heart stalled. The wide funnel was weaving and twisting and dancing its way toward him, oblivious to the trees and other landmarks in its way.

Adrenaline his guide, aided by pure instinct, Jack stumbled forward, half running, half crawling toward the doomed building. "Carillon!" he screamed, his voice now hoarse with the effort.

Then his breath was gone.

He couldn't move.

Splaying himself out onto the ground, he tried to lift his head, but branches, chunks of wood, and other items he couldn't even identify kept hurtling past him. He ducked his head, dodged a piece, and lifted it up once more, watching helplessly as the sinister cloud advanced.

One more time. He lifted a knee, trying to get into a hands-and-knees position — and was knocked flat with a wicked slap to his side. Grimacing at the sharp pain in his ribs, he turned and watched a substantial beam flying end over end. With a groan, he flattened himself on the ground once more. "Father," he croaked, "again . . . You kn– know where . . . she is." Even the effort to speak hurt. He closed his eyes. *Wrap Your arms around her. Protect her, Lord. Draw her close to You.*

At that moment, an earsplitting explosion of wood, glass, and other material showered the tense air around him.

Barely able to lift his head, he looked up and ahead.

The teacherage was gone. Gone.

A lump grew in his throat and he buried his head back in the wet grass. But the grief was quickly taken over by panic as he felt himself rising off the ground. Battling for what he knew could very well be his life, he thrashed against the force trying to suck him from the earth. Each movement brought the same stabbing pain to his side and somewhere deeper inside his chest.

Trying to inch, crawl, scramble — anything. Anything to escape from the invisible clutches of the tornado's talons.

In a split second, he felt himself drop back to the unforgiving dirt below, the cavernous suction still stealing his breath. *It must be moving away — in the other direction.* That was his last thought before a chunk of debris slammed viciously against his skull.

For the briefest of seconds, he felt no more pain. Only a dizzying warmth. A muted comfort. A stillness. Then everything became blackness.

How long they'd been in the root cellar, Carillon couldn't begin to guess. Ten minutes? Ten years?

The resounding roar had abated quite awhile ago, and now the only discernible sound from the other side of the door was the subtle patter of rain. Paul was the first to stand up. None of the others seemed eager to join him. Taking his leadership role seriously, he headed to the door, slowly unlatched it, and peered hesitantly up from the bottom of the steps. After a second or two, he started up, his legs then his feet disappearing as he went higher. Everyone else was silent. Anxious.

After a minute or two had passed, some of them started to squirm. "Paul?" one of the guys called out. "Paul, what's out there?"

After a moment, Paul's feet reappeared on the stairs. Each person eagerly watched as his face came into view. Their eagerness fell into subtle despair when they saw his countenance.

"You can come out now," he said quietly. "It's over."

Their legs wobbly from fear and from sitting so long, the small group rose to its feet, timidly following the blacksmith out and up into the slowly abating rain.

The first thing that met them was the huge oak, sprawled literally only feet away from the house like some felled giant. Under its mass of crushed leaves and branches lay what remained of the carriage house.

A few gasps were heard behind Carillon — along with a few whispers of thanks to God that the tree hadn't hit the house proper.

But then their eyes shifted to take in the entire town.

Or rather, what was left of it.

The general store had shifted off its foundation, its sides bent at an awkward angle, looking like a toy building made of matchsticks that had been stepped on by a child. The boardinghouse had no windows intact, and the roof looked like someone had peeled off most of the shingles. But the worst site was the blacksmith shop and livery stable.

They were gone.

All that remained was the erect stone chimney of Paul's fireplace.

Carillon heard several sniffles behind her. She, herself, was still too stunned to register much of any emotion.

"Look!" someone cried.

All the others turned to where they were pointing. There, at the far end of the main street, unscathed by the battle that had just occurred, stood the church. Proud and patrician. Graceful and resolute.

Several in the crowd headed in its direction. More began to follow.

But Carillon hesitated, her eyes wanting to turn the other way — over the field and through the battered woods.

Paul must have sensed her hesitation. She found him standing at her side looking down at her, his eyes full of understanding. "Shall we go and check things out?"

Taking a deep breath, Carillon nodded. "I just want to make sure he's okay."

He tossed off the blanket still hanging over his shoulders. "All right. You head to his cabin. I'll go and see about your place."

Giving him a weak smile, she threw off her own wrap and started down the gravel road, the only sound between them, the crunch of their feet on the wet stones. She found herself praying again. *Please . . . please let him be all right.*

By the time she and Paul split up to take the separate paths, Carillon was nearly at Jack's cabin. Unconsciously holding her breath, she rounded the corner to the clearing. Never before had she felt such relief.

The barn stood strong. All the other buildings remained intact. The cabin had not been bothered an iota. Closing her eyes in thankfulness, her steps quickened as she approached the cabin. "Jack!"

The front door gaped open. Skittering up the steps, she stood in the kitchen, noticing the floor was wet. Apparently the door had blown open during the storm. "Jack? Are you in here?"

No answer.

Sense coming to her, she realized exactly where he'd be. Outside. Checking the buildings. The animals.

She raced to the barn. "Jack?"

Only the nervously twitching cows and horses stared at her.

The chicken house? Not there, either.

She stood in the middle of the yard and slowly turned around. "Jack?" Why she kept calling, she didn't know. It was obvious he wasn't there.

The only other place he might be — Of course, he'd have headed to the compound . . . or even Liberty Town to survey the damage everywhere else. It's what he would do.

Taking a relaxing breath, she started back toward the path that led toward the town again. Halfway there, curiosity got the better of her. What about the school? The teacherage?

Frowning, she looked from the one trail to the other. She could just check on it quickly, then head back.

Before her mind had completely made itself up, she saw a figure approaching under the shadow of the trees from the path leading to her place. Ready to call out Jack's name, she held her tongue when she realized it wasn't him.

Paul emerged, his face an ashen white.

Carillon scurried over to him. "What? Is it the school?"

He shook his head. "The school is . . . beat up. But okay."

"The teacherage?"

"Gone," he said hoarsely.

"Gone?" Her mind refused to grasp the immensity of the statement. "Gone?" She looked past his shoulder and started to walk around him.

He grabbed her arm and held it fast.

Surprised at his sudden grip, she met his eyes and frowned. "I want to see. I can handle it —"

Paul shook his head again. "Jack's back there." His voice was barely above a whisper.

"What?"

A surprising pool of tears welled up in the young man's eyes.

"What?" Her eyes darted to the path again. "What do you mean, Jack's back there?" She started forward again.

He tightened his grip on her arm.

"Paul! What do you mean? Is he okay? Is he hurt? What . . ." Her words died away as she watched his face contort in an effort to control a sob.

Hot tears sprang to her own eyes, spilling down her cheeks maddeningly. "What's the matter?" she demanded angrily. She didn't understand her anger or who it might be directed at. She just knew she was overwhelmed with rage. "What's happened?"

Paul could only shake his head as his lower lip quivered.

Carillon grabbed his immense shoulders and shook them with all her strength. "Where is Jack? Is he all right?"

He sniffed and swiped a large palm over his eyes. "I don't know. Bob and some of the other guys were already there. They've called for an ambulance."

"An ambulance?" Horror squeezed her lungs and her heart. "Paul, tell me."

Paul gazed off toward the teacherage. "He wasn't moving. He was on the ground, and he wasn't moving."

The words buzzed around in her head — around and around and around. They were making her dizzy. Sick.

She, too, looked down the seemingly

peaceful trail, fraudulently disguised under the now calm trees. It became a tunnel — the edges getting fuzzier and fuzzier, fading to black. To black.

To nothingness . . .

# Chapter 17

Complete and total exhaustion drained the life from her body in a way Carillon had never experienced before. If the events of the last twenty-four hours weren't enough, their staggering repercussions were.

Reeling in shock, along with everyone else at Yesteryear, she'd taken the trek to the hospital with a small group of people. Yet when she'd walked into Jack's room, for some ridiculous reason, she was totally unprepared for what she saw.

The myriad of tubes and wires taped to his pale, still frame nearly sent her over the edge. It was too much. Flickering in and out of her wavering consciousness as she stared at him were images of Evie. . . .

A flurry of doctors and nurses surrounded Carillon's little sister. Orders being called out — the tone direct, but quiet.

Her parents finally at her side. Carillon feeling a world away from them — and wishing she were twice that far away physically if only to escape the intense guilt and shame smothering her.

Back at Jack's room, someone had the presence of mind to grab a chair and usher her into it.

Everything else seemed so surreal. This couldn't be happening, could it? What seemed only hours ago, they'd been together on the little boat. Now here he was unconscious in a hospital bed. His future? None of the doctors seemed to want to speculate. The terms "possible brain injury" and "further tests" kept coming around, but nothing more definite than that.

In her hands, Carillon clutched the few things she'd brought with her, the only things that seemed of any importance anymore. Amazingly, in the midst of the rubble surrounding what had been the teacherage, she'd found Madeline's journal and Bible intact, as well as the journal from Jack.

She stared down at the volumes now.

Everyone else had vacated the room. Why, she wasn't sure, but she suspected that Paul's prompting had something to do with it. So other than the beep and hiss of machines floating amid the subdued aura of the ICU, it remained quiet. She wondered what on earth to do. To say. The nurses had encouraged them all to talk to Jack, reminding them that often those in a coma can still hear, still comprehend.

She had planned to read some of Madeline's entries to him because she couldn't come up with any words of her own. Not any that wouldn't cause excruciating pain — or more guilt. In the back of her mind, Carillon couldn't forget that the reason Jack Tate was lying in this hospital room, vacillating between life and death, was because of her. Plain and simple.

Here it was all over again.

The same reason Evie had slipped away from her . . . it was all her fault.

By the time Bob came to tell her it was time to go, she'd spent the entire fifteen minutes saying nothing, barely able to keep her eyes focused on his face. Occasionally she had reached over and tentatively touched his hand, his fingers. They felt so cold. So unlike him . . .

It had been the ride home in the large van that put the quintessential cap on this day. In the midst of the chaos surrounding Yesteryear's sudden need for closure, the employees and visitors found themselves faced with the question of where to go next — and when. For the majority of them, their only choice was returning home.

Carillon couldn't comprehend their eagerness. Each, in spite of the disappointment of a short season and the worry surrounding Jack, seemed relieved at the prospect of heading for home.

Was that her only choice? Would her parents show up to retrieve her? To take her back to wherever they lived now? During the few months Carillon had been gone, her parents had managed to sell their house — the one with so many bad memories — and locate elsewhere. Closer to church, they'd said. Carillon hadn't responded. Did it really matter where they lived? It would change nothing. Undo nothing.

If that possible scenario wasn't enough to keep her brain busy, Bob had blown her out of the water with his own request — to look after Jack's cabin until he came back. Carillon didn't miss the hopeful optimism in his voice. Nor did he seem to miss what must have been obvious doubt flickering in her eyes.

"Are you sure?" she stammered. "I mean, Paul . . . or somebody else could —"

"Paul has agreed to do the outside chores. But he's staying at the compound, helping tally the lists for replacement and repair costs." The large man's face looked anxious. "If you wouldn't mind?"

Carillon tried not to sigh too loudly as she directed her gaze out at the drizzly day. "All right," she agreed quietly. "I'll try."

Bob clapped a large hand over hers in gratitude. "Thank you, Carillon."

Now here she was.

And it was the worst mistake she'd made thus far in her short life.

Sliding her arms across the wooden table, she let her head flop down on them, the painful lump in her throat so thick it burned with every swallow. "What are you doing?" she whispered to the silence in the little cabin. The little place that personified Jack.

She'd managed to clean up the kitchen and living area mechanically, washing, drying, stacking, sweeping — grateful for how quickly it made the time pass. But now . . . now the sun had sunk behind the horizon, the flicker of the lantern cast wavering shadows across the log walls, and the doubts and fears and inadequacies were finding her again.

Lifting her chin wearily, she stared at the sturdily made ladder that led up to Jack's sleeping area. His own personal place. The yawning black space above gaped down at her, almost daring her to invade it.

Closing her eyes, she rested her forehead against the table again. She'd made a stupid, stupid mistake. Again. She'd promised to do something more than she could.

Another hollow word to add to her list.

But where else could she go?

Trying to will her nerves into some sort of resolve, she stood and gripped the handle of the lantern in one hand and placed a somewhat shaky grip on the rung of the ladder.

Boosting herself up, she climbed. Step after step, rung after rung, as the orangish light slowly ate up the darkness above her.

Reaching the top, she stepped onto the loft's platform, surprised at the generous-sized room. Bookcases dominated one whole side of the loft. In spite of herself, Carillon couldn't contain the little smile. Of course. Jack would have scads of books.

The end, under the steep dormer, housed a small window looking to the woods beyond. The wall opposite the bookshelves left enough room for a goodly sized cot and a small bedside table and chair.

Carillon stared at the small bed, its sheets and blankets still mussed from the last night of sleep. Jack's sleep. Inching toward it, she hesitantly reached out a hand, smoothing the edge of the thick blanket. Easing to her knees, she straightened the bedclothes and finally grabbed the feather pillow, fluffing it gently as she replaced it at the head. With each movement, each tuck, the subtle scent of Jack greeted her senses. A soulful combination of fresh air, wood smoke, and soap.

The choking lump in her throat grew larger still, and her eyes burned with threatening tears. Turning her back on the bunk, she focused her attention instead on the books. Read. Maybe that would help. She must get her mind focused on something else — anything else — until she was ready to drop off to sleep immediately. But even then, she had no clue how she was going to manage sliding into Jack Tate's bed and sleeping peacefully.

For the moment, she concentrated on the stacks and stacks of volumes before her. Lots of classics. Lots. But nothing that really grabbed her attention. Her finger trailed along the worn edges of the leather spines, hesitating every few titles.

Then she came to the end of the top shelf. The huge book had to be at least four inches thick. Hefting it from its place, she blinked at the cover.

Holy Bible.

Settling onto the floor, she tugged it onto her lap and peeled open the crackling cover. Within the first few thick, yellowed pages were a myriad of handwritten words in aged, blue ink. Obviously in some other language — German, from the look of it.

Intrigued, she continued. She came to a

series of pages with a distinct pattern of neat, heavy lines. Each one held a name, a date, sometimes a note.

A family tree of sorts.

Glancing at the first entry she came to, she sobered. *Byron Alvin Tate, died March 4, 1992.* She swallowed. Jack had mentioned that his parents had died, but reading it in Jack's neat hand somehow made it harder to think about.

*Alice Marie Tate, died July 7, 1989.* His mother. Her heart ached for him.

Then, smiling a little shakily, she touched the following words: *Jack William Tate, born August 20, 1974.* They were written in a neat, feminine script she assumed to belong to Jack's mother. She went on.

*Jonathon Byron Tate, born November 17, 1969.* Her heart chilled for a fraction, until she reread it and imagined the posting being entered by a new mother on the birth of her firstborn son. What hopes and dreams had she had for her sons?

*Byron Alvin Tate and Alice Marie Henrikson, married June 30, 1968.* Jack's parents. Byron and Alice.

Carillon started to move on — then looked back. Zeroing in on Alice's name. Henrikson. Odd. She remembered Madeline Whitcomb's farmer . . . William

Henrikson. It had to be coincidence. Henrikson was a common enough name.

Even if Jack's middle name was William also?

Her breath quickening, she slid her finger down the continuing list of names, through WWII, through the Great Depression, through the turn of the century. The name Henrikson remained a mainstay in the genealogy from Jack's mother back.

The list grew shorter and shorter as she flipped through the pages of birth dates, children, marriages, deaths. Then she came to the final entry among the pages, the one that signaled the beginning of the record keeping. Her heart stalled.

*William Peder Henrikson and Madeline Sarah Whitcomb, married August 3, 1854.*

No way. This was not possible. It just couldn't —

Carillon shoved the book off her lap and scrambled back down the ladder to where she'd left the journals on the table. Scooping them up and trotting up the rungs again, she plopped next to the still-open Bible and began flipping through Madeline's journal. She'd almost read the entire thing. Almost.

But for now, she flipped straight to the end, finding the last few entries.

Eighteen fifty-four . . . Spring, spring, end of school year . . . here it was — summer.

*8 June 1854*

*The school year is finished. I survived!*

*The children brought me an assortment of lovely wildflowers and miscellaneous candies and baked goodies today. On several occasions I had to rein myself in so as not to show too much emotion in front of them. It was both a good and rather difficult day.*

*I received a letter from Mother and Father today. Even Father seems surprised at my success in having completed the year "unscathed." I penned them a letter back almost immediately. Partially to tell them of my final day at this charming little school — that thought still brings tears to my eyes at times. I think I could stay . . . if there were not future plans with which to contend.*

*As my parents will make their trek out here to help retrieve some of my things, I think — no, I know — they will be much surprised when we pick them up at the station . . . William and I.*

*For William has a particular question he wants to ask of my father.*

*And it's that thought alone that thrills me . . . and makes the giving up of this teaching position a rather small thing to bear. For if our plans go as we hope, within a few short months, I will be Mrs. William Henrikson — and quite possibly the most blessed and happy woman on this earth.*

Carillon let the diary slip from her hands to the floor, landing next to the family Bible.

Somewhere in the lineage, Madeline was Jack's however-many-great-grandmother. All the treks Carillon had made from that same teacherage to that same farm to see a descendant of the Henrikson name . . .

It was too unreal. What kind of fate would allow this to happen? And with such a cruel ending?

Whatever the reason Carillon had ended up here, she knew it was no longer her place to stay. She could not stay and dare to hope that her future lay anywhere in the same vicinity as people like the faithful Madeline

Whitcomb or the equally righteous Jack Tate.

Probably, she'd already stayed too long. She'd already messed things up. She'd taken away whatever good life Jack might have had. All because of her.

Taking labored breaths, she glanced around the cabin, feeling the age-old oppression ever creeping in on her.

Leaving the Bible, the journal . . . even Jack's gift, she grabbed the lantern, descended quietly to the kitchen, and strode out the door.

Shirking her responsibility to Bob? Probably.

But in the long run, he'd thank her. No one needed her kind of help around.

The kind that only seems to take, take, take.

Evie was gone.

Jack was going.

And Carillon wasn't going to be there to watch it. Not this time.

# Chapter 18

*Two months later*

Jack reached up and ruffled the short, spiky hair that had grown back after they'd shaved his head . . . or so he'd been told. Along with everything else in his immediate past, the memory of that event was gone. He relied on the reports of doctors, nurses, friends — and the disjointed memories. The last thing he remembered was running toward the teacherage, calling her name.

His heart panged. Even the briefest reminder brought a piercing to his gut.

Fairly unaware when he'd finally come out of his coma, it had taken him some time to orient himself. A regular flow of visitors eased the transition as he watched the faces from his past float into his present. All but that one.

He could only assume that she'd gone. That left the greatest hollowness within him. No one mentioned her. At all. Other than to assure him, somewhat hesitantly, that Carillon was all right . . . she'd not been injured in the storm. Then the subject quickly shifted to the repairs and rebuilding being done at Yesteryear. With some frustration, Jack had listened, unable to voice his further questions, concerns.

It seemed the shocking blow given his brain had produced a few changes. To his amazement, the stutter was gone. But in its place, giving him equal, if not more frustration, was his occasional inability to properly voice his thoughts. Where before the words had stumbled around on his tongue in an effort to get out, now they were elusive — hiding in some secret, locked part of his mind that gave no rhyme or reason to when and where it would act up.

The doctor assured him this was normal and that most likely, with time, his language skills would return.

In the meantime, he sat in the stiff hospital bed, counting the days until he might be released, eager to get back to the little cabin. And wondering what the future might hold now.

His thoughts were in that very place the afternoon that Bob Feldman came to see him. Jack had been busy studying the changing leaves outside the window, the last of the colored remnants stubbornly clinging to otherwise bare branches.

"Jack!"

He turned with a smile and greeted the jovial man. "Hi, Bob."

Shrugging out of his ample jacket, Bob grinned as he plopped down a new set of books to occupy Jack. "Maybe by the time you finish these, they'll let you out of here."

"We can only hope," Jack muttered, perusing the titles.

"Well, that and guests should keep you busy."

Jack inclined his head. "Yeah? I've actually been tempted to start watching Oprah." He nodded at the television mounted to the wall.

Bob let out a low breath. "I'll talk to the doctor today."

They smiled at one another as Jack adjusted himself in the propped-up bed, grabbing the stack of books.

"Uh . . . Jack?"

He kept rummaging through the volumes. "Yeah?"

"There's someone here to see you."

Jack lifted his eyes and studied his ill-at-ease friend. Maybe it was Bob's tone. Or his hesitancy. Whatever, it grabbed him, causing him to struggle to continue suppressing the hopes he'd been harboring since he woke up those many weeks ago.

"They've come a ways."

They?

From the corner of his eye, Jack saw subtle movement beyond the glass window of his room's door. "Who is it?"

Bob slowly cracked the knuckles of his short, thick fingers. "Mr. and Mrs. DeVries."

Boom. Just like that. And not at all what he'd expected, if he'd expected anything. "They want to see me?"

Bob nodded and shot a look over his shoulder at the closed door.

Suddenly self-conscious, Jack ran a hand across his head again, hoping to smooth down any errant cowlicks. Bob didn't say that Carillon was with them. But what if . . .

"Is that all right?"

Jack nodded and pulled himself straighter in the bed, smoothing the wrinkled sheets.

Bob rose from the low chair, crossed to the door, and opened it a fraction, sticking his head out into the hall and beckoning with his arm. Within a matter of seconds, Jack found himself face-to-face with Carillon's parents.

Stunned, he immediately recognized that she'd been a perfect composite of the older couple, with her mother's small build and coloring and her father's regal features. Jack suddenly realized that he was staring.

Thankfully, Bob broke the somewhat uncomfortable silence. "Mr. and Mrs. DeVries, this is Jack Tate. Jack, Mr. and Mrs. DeVries."

They nodded at one another as each of them reached forward and cordially shook hands.

"Curtis," her father corrected with a friendly smile.

"And Rachel," his wife added.

"Nice to meet you."

"Here," Bob interjected. "You two have a seat." He pushed up another chair. "I'm gonna go see what's for lunch today." With a broad smile, he waved and backed out of the room, pulling the door shut behind him.

Jack nodded after him.

For several seconds, the two parties simply looked at one another, the discomfort and uneasiness palpable. Curtis finally broke it. "I understand you were trying to save Carillon when the tornado hit."

Studying his hands with a slight frown, Jack shrugged his shoulders. "I didn't know she wasn't there."

"We appreciate your efforts," Rachel added. "All of them."

His gaze snapped up to theirs.

"Mr. Feldman has told us some of what you did . . . and what you tried to do for our daughter," Curtis said. "We really can't express our gratitude."

With a quiet smile, Jack felt his heart soften. "She's . . . all right then?"

The couple looked at one another. Curtis spoke again. "We don't know."

Jack was puzzled by his response.

"We haven't seen her since she left for Yesteryear."

"What?" He sat up straight again, momentarily wincing at the pain that surged through his ribs now and again. "But I thought —"

Rachel shook her head. "She never came home. We don't know where she is."

With a long breath, Jack flopped back against the pillows and shut his eyes. Where on earth had she gone? What was she doing? Was she all right? Somewhere in the midst of his selfish concerns, he remembered whom he was sitting next to. He peeled open his eyes and found them looking at him. "I'm sorry," he murmured. "It must be very . . . painful to not know where your daughter is."

Rachel DeVries's eyes clouded with tears. "I'm afraid we haven't known where our daughter has been for a number of years."

Jack studied them, confused.

Curtis grabbed his wife's hand and squeezed it tightly. "Did Carillon mention anything to you? Anything at all?"

"About?"

"Us?"

Jack shook his head. "Nothing other than how she got her name."

"Her sister?"

Again, he shook his head. "She didn't seem eager to share much of anything."

Curtis sighed heavily. "I'm afraid that's probably our fault. You see, we haven't exactly been the best . . . example."

"Of . . . ?"

"Christians."

"Both of us were saved about five years ago," Rachel explained, seeming to have gotten the tears under control. "We were ecstatic in this new hope we found in Jesus. Our pasts wiped clean, our futures bright with His promise."

Jack nodded in understanding.

"Carillon, though, was less than thrilled with our newfound faith. She was fifteen, full of a bit of normal teenage rebellion, and not real eager to be attending church every night of the week. It seems we did find something to keep us at the church almost every night. She didn't understand it. And we didn't understand her hesitancy."

"We see now," Curtis offered, "that we neglected our responsibilities as parents in lieu of trying to do everything with our new family at the church. Given Carillon's age and mind-set, we needed wisdom and patience in how to show her our faith without totally ramrodding it down her throat. We could have done far more by simply loving her, rather than pointing out all of her shortcomings when stacked up against our new expectations."

Jack sighed, finally understanding the young woman's attitude, fear, and seeming callousness. But at the same time he felt genuine regret and compassion for the couple before him. He knew the last thing they'd wanted to do was lose their daughter. By the looks of things, it seemed that's exactly what had happened. His mind turning over past events and memories, one question shot to the forefront. "What happened to your other daughter?" he asked quietly, carefully.

"Evie?" Rachel inquired.

Again, they sought one another's eyes before Curtis took the cue. "Last May, just before Carillon came here to Yesteryear, Evie drowned in our swimming pool."

The ache in Jack's heart settled into a

sickening lump in his stomach. "How old was she?"

"Six."

Feeling the profound sorrow emanating from these parents, he simply waited, realizing their need for space, time.

"What made it worse," Curtis continued, his voice husky with emotion, "was that Carillon was home, baby-sitting her." He again squeezed Rachel's hand, as the tears freely fell down her fair cheeks. "We know that Carillon blames herself. She didn't ever say much to us, but it seemed . . . it seemed as though she felt that anyone she would get close to . . . would die."

Jack nodded, the final pieces fitting together. Her self-made walls. Her animosity used to fortify those walls. Her distance fueled by the fear of getting close to anyone. And now — now she was gone.

"Jack?" Rachel sniffled.

Trying to ignore the tightness pressing against his chest, he turned toward the woman.

"Do you know," she pleaded, "do you have any idea where she might have gone? Did she ever say anything to you about leaving?"

With the most severe case of regret he'd ever felt, Jack slowly shook his head. "No. She never did."

Unable to stifle the sob, Rachel shook under its quiet intensity. Her husband wrapped his arm around her shoulders, trying to console her while his own face held the most piteous look of grief that Jack had seen in a long, long while.

Lost in the discomfort of the moment, Jack sank into the background until that inner urge spurred him to action. He studied the couple before him, then swallowed hard. "Uh . . . would you mind . . ."

The two faces peered up at him.

"If we prayed?" he finished the question.

Nodding, they gripped each others' hands, stood, and took Jack's outstretched ones.

Jack closed his eyes, released a deep breath, and settled in. "Father, You know why we're here today. . . ."

The warmth of the Ozark sun permeated the cab of the huge semi, the rolling landscape temporarily lost on Carillon as she stared out the window, seeing nothing and feeling everything. The roar of the air-conditioning and quiet banter of the radio filled in the otherwise quiet space. That was fine with her. She'd had a hard enough time deciding whether or not to take this particular ride — scintillating conversation she didn't need.

But glancing again at Ralph — whom she'd known for about, oh, three hours now — she realized for once she had nothing to fear. Other than fear itself. She smiled inwardly at the irony.

If her mind had been a whirling vortex of confusion the last couple of months, the last few hours would have to top it all. She tried to piece together the avenues that had gotten her here . . . sitting in this strange rig with a man who defied all stereotypes of truckers she'd ever heard about.

Her night-covered departure from Yesteryear was somewhat of a blur. All she knew was she'd ended up near an interstate highway, her small duffel of belongings slung over her shoulder. Somehow, between good-hearted citizens who probably thought she was a mere kid scraping together enough fare for a long, bumpy bus ride, Carillon had found herself traveling farther and farther away from that place. From home. From all that she no longer wanted — nor wanted to remember.

Two months. Eight and a half solid weeks had elapsed when she ended up near Branson, Missouri, and then found her way to a YWCA where she could at least shower, change clothes, and sleep for a pittance. But after a time she questioned what she was doing. What kind of a life was this? And for how long could it last? She needed to at least find a job. Anything.

After having grown accustomed to the peacefulness of Yesteryear, she began hiking out of the city of Branson to the outskirts — some of the smaller towns that lay in the highway's path. Seeing a large truck stop, she gratefully went in, counted out the money she had, bought a meager meal, and inquired about possible positions available for waitressing — or anything else.

Needing help, they hired her on the spot. Carillon felt good that she was on her way to independence, and she concentrated on her job. Doing it well. Doing it constantly. Working double shifts whenever possible just to avoid the time alone, the time for her thoughts to revert back to people and places she had no right to be dwelling on.

But more than once she'd almost dropped her platter of dishes when, from across the dining room, she'd spotted that golden-brown hair . . . the slight build. Her heart lodged in her throat when he turned around to reveal a face entirely too different — disappointingly so.

And in the aftermath that always occurred, she found herself battling bizarre longings. Desires to go home. To head back to the upper Midwest. To what she knew. To what might have been — even if it would never be.

But the desires disappeared as she counted out her skimpy tips, realizing there was no way she would get back to Wisconsin or Minnesota on this wage. Then the bitterness and misery set in. She knew she had no one to blame but herself, as always. But she was also beginning to wonder if God had a personal vendetta against her.

What made it worse was the realization that she'd landed right smack dab on the buckle of the Bible belt. On more than one occasion, she'd have to endure invitations from her coworkers to attend their church. She always found excuses — even if they weren't particularly imaginative.

But God never let her go. She could feel it. And she chafed under the discomfort. She wanted to be left alone. What started as a relieving cry of freedom had now turned into a continual ache. One that wouldn't go away. If she'd been miserable before, each day took Carillon well past that edge, making her wonder how she'd hang on.

It had been today's lunch rush that had harried her the most. It seemed a zillion people came and went. Hundreds of seniors on their way to their southern winter homes and twice that many headed for the entertainment capital of Branson kept the place packed. And of course there were the usual hosts of truck drivers.

When the final flow had ebbed a bit, Carillon had taken two seconds to sit in an empty booth, grab a sandwich, and rub her aching legs. Letting her gaze follow the continuous maze of traffic to the restaurant and gas pumps outside, she felt a chunk of the sandwich lodge funnily in her throat.

From across the crowded lot, a truck barreled into a parking stall. And into her brain.

The front grill of the huge Peterbilt was adorned with the most unusual ornament she'd seen — and she'd seen some unusual ones. But this one . . .

The neon blue light glowing to beat the bright sunshine, the shape unmistakably fashioned into a cross.

Carillon frowned at the image.

She watched as a middle-aged, normal-looking guy hopped down from the cab, waved at a couple of truckers who were fueling up, and proceeded into the restaurant. Unable to take her eyes off him because of her curiosity, she jumped when Charlotte had nudged her elbow.

"Hey, Doll," she'd said with a weary smile. "You mind taking over for me for a bit? I have to pick up Billy from his dad's all of a sudden and take him to the sitter's."

Carillon nodded, cleared her basket, and smoothed her apron. She watched as the cross guy settled into Charlotte's section.

"Thanks," her coworker mumbled, digging her keys out of her purse and striding out the door.

Feeling an odd sense of apprehension, Carillon snatched up a menu from the holder and strode over to the man. "Good afternoon," she offered.

He smiled at her. "It is that. Nice day today."

No accent. She noticed that right away. Nodding with a polite smile, she placed the menu in front of him and ran off to fetch him a hot cup of coffee.

By the time she returned, he rattled off his order quickly and efficiently.

"Boy, that was fast," she admitted, scribbling down the order. "You must be in a hurry today."

He grinned and took a sip of the steaming liquid. "Sure am. Heading home tonight."

"Ah." She knew that was always a cause for good-spirited truckers. "Where's

240

home?" she asked by way of conversation.

"St. Paul."

Her pencil ground to a stop on the little pad, snapping the lead.

She was sure he had noticed her reaction when he eyed her and asked, "Heard of it?"

Keeping her eyes glued on the writing in front of her, she nodded. "Sure." With that, she stuck the order slip on the merry-go-round for the cooks and went to check on any other jobs she might be able to accomplish — if only to avoid the unsettled feeling she got while around this new customer. Maybe Annie needed help refilling the ketchup bottles.

"Got it covered," she informed Carillon.

There weren't many options left. Other than ones right around Mr. Cross.

Steeling herself against her ridiculous nerves, Carillon returned and began wiping down the counters around his stool. She saw him watching her. Not leering, but studying.

When his order came up, she placed it in front of him with her usual smile.

"Looks terrific." He smiled in return. Then he bowed his head and prayed silently.

Unable to tear her eyes from him, Carillon watched his silent conversation with God.

When he'd finished, he lifted his head . . . and noticed her staring. He tilted his head slightly in question, his brows lifted.

Feeling her face heat in embarrassment, Carillon tried to think of something to say just to break the awkwardness of the moment. "Why do you have a cross on your truck?" she blurted out.

He smiled. "I'd love to tell you about it."

The remainder of the day was a blur now. An obscure cacophony of memories, feelings of homesickness, the unusual story of this man's ministry, Truckers for Christ, and the shocking question this complete stranger had posed before he'd left.

"I feel like I'm supposed to ask you something," he said while paying his bill.

"What's that?" Carillon asked with more than a little apprehension.

"I feel like I'm supposed to ask you if —" He broke off with a huff of amusement. Or maybe it was his own hesitation. He cleared his throat. "I'm supposed to ask you if you want to go home."

Carillon didn't remember her reaction — or how long it took. She just remembered the dizzying, overwhelming feeling that came over her as she placed her apron on the back counter and told Joe, the cook, that she wouldn't be back tomorrow. Or again.

As she sat in the cab of the truck, reviewing her day, Carillon felt an overpowering sense of fear, apprehension . . . and peace.

Somehow, deep inside, she knew. It was time to go home.

# Chapter 19

Jack stared out at the drizzly day, the wet road beneath him, and the choppy Mississippi lining his route. He'd been on the road for several hours now, yet each mile that brought him closer to his destination increasingly filled him with trepidation. That he was doing the right thing, he had no doubt. Doubt was one issue he didn't seem to struggle with much anymore. He'd been shown that in quick order over these last weeks and months. Life was too short. And he knew now, when God directed — you went.

That had brought Jack to his first decision.

After his release from the hospital, he'd reveled in walking the paths of Yesteryear again, even though things had changed subtly. He'd watched Paul and some of the others lending a hand when the carpenters came in to start rebuilding the lost and damaged property. And entering his own cabin . . . it had been bittersweet. Full of good memories, comfortable. Yet filled with painful reminders as well. Namely, Carillon's journal still lying in his loft. Unopened. Blank. Next to it, the family Bible and his distant relative's own journal — amazing that they had survived not only the tornado but also all those years in waiting. Perhaps waiting for someone to find it? Someone . . .

He prayed for her constantly. Wherever she might be. And hoped that those simple prayers would be enough not only to sustain her, but to sustain him, as well, and fill the emptiness left by her departure.

His trek to the old farmstead had probably given him the biggest shock, though. Stepping into the clearing, he'd blinked . . . then blinked again at the gaping space.

The house was gone. The barn, gone. Not a trace of anything save the debris littering the rain-beaten grasses. In that instant of sorrow and relief, Jack knew. He knew without a doubt what he was supposed to do both immediately and long-term.

It was the immediate directive that found him now driving in Bob's truck, heading down the highway to a place he'd never been. A river town called Prairie du Chien.

By the time he'd passed all the locks and dams dotting the Mississippi's long descent along Wisconsin's western border and found himself rolling into the quaint but busy place, he pulled into a gas station, refueling the small pickup. He paid for his purchases and cleared his throat, eyeing the attendant. "Could you tell me how to get to the prison?"

The lady's carefully penciled-in brows lifted a fraction. "The max one?"

He nodded.

She leaned over the counter, pointing out the window, rattling off street names and numbers of blocks.

He nodded his thanks and stepped out into the cold, rainy October day. Easing into the cab, he took a deep breath, let it out slowly, and closed his eyes. "Okay, Father. Here we go. I can't do this without You." Twisting the key in the ignition, he popped the truck into gear and set out down the road.

"Are you sure?" he'd asked for the hundredth time. "I know Deb wouldn't mind if you stayed with us — even for just a few days."

Carillon nodded, reassuring him. "I'll be fine." She hoisted the duffel farther up on her shoulder and reached out a hand. "Thank you, Ralph. For everything."

He gripped hers in return and smiled. "Jesus will be at your side, Carillon, every step of the way."

She nodded, trying not to let the tears choke her up again. "I think I kind of know that now," she whispered. "Someone else told me that quite awhile ago. I just need to find Him."

"No," Ralph answered, "He's already here. Don't go looking. Just meet Him where you are."

She frowned a little, but nodded anyway. "Good-bye. And thanks again."

He released her hand and gave her a confident smile. "We'll be praying for you."

She waved over her shoulder and started toward the nearest bus stop. With the little money she'd managed to bring, along with a hefty chunk of Ralph's he had insisted she keep, she could afford a few short fares. After that? She didn't know. She guessed she'd cross that bridge later.

The huge city bus hissed to a stop in front of her, its door sliding open to allow her refuge from the damp day. She plopped the required fare into the box and found a seat near the back, settling onto the cold vinyl bench as the roar of the engine inched the vehicle forward, taking Carillon to a different place and time. To a place where she hoped to find . . . something. Peace? Closure? That part was unclear yet. And it scared her more than a little.

They let him in quickly enough. He'd had the foresight to call several days before and set up an appointment. After the guard at the front verified who he was, Jack found himself following another armed guard through a maze of hallways, double-thick steel doors, and security gates. Some corridors were eerily quiet; others ricocheted with the voices of men in the midst of some activity or another.

After several minutes, Jack was led to a small room with a table and a few chairs. Heavy, black iron bars girded the few windows letting in the meager light from the gray day.

"Have a seat, Mr. Tate," the guard informed him. "I'll let 'em know you're ready."

He nodded and opted to stay standing, crossing to the windows, clutching his Bible with renewed intensity. Staring down at the courtyard, he felt that sick feeling rise from the pit of his stomach again. The space outdoors was empty in the inclement weather. But the grass was nicely trimmed. The paved area showed no immediate signs of disrepair. Several basketball hoops flanked the ends of the yard. It looked like an overgrown playground, minus the equipment.

Until one looked at its perimeters.

Lining the seemingly pristine grounds, huge chain-link fences rose to towering heights. Not one, but two fences followed each other in a parallel pattern, completely encasing the area surrounding all of the prison. If the height of the fences alone wasn't enough deterrent against escape attempts, several feet of wicked razor wire twisted and coiled sharply in an intimidating cap on the barrier. The mere sight of it chilled him. It brought back memories of pictures he'd seen of the concentration camps during World War II. Only this time the barriers weren't to keep people in because of one sick man's desire to rid the earth of all he deemed inferior. These barriers protected those on the outside from the sickness and sin that permeated the people held in this place.

The door latch clicked open behind him. Jack jumped and turned around to see two guards leading a man in.

Jon.

Jack felt that lump rising in his throat, and he battled to swallow it again. He needed to be strong.

It had been many, many years. He was still big. Jack didn't have to guess that he probably made use of the weight room. But his muscular arms and legs were somewhat hidden under the required uniform he wore. His ankles were cuffed and chained, his arms secured tightly behind his back as well. It was odd to see him so . . . subdued. His hair was still the same shade as Jack's, albeit with a few gray strands poking through. His face . . . Jack couldn't see. So far Jon kept his head toward the floor.

The guards assisted Jon to a chair, and Jack released a breath, slowly approaching the opposite side of the table. "About fifteen minutes," one of them said as they retreated through the door.

"Wait."

They turned, eyeing Jack expectantly.

He nodded toward his brother. "Could you at least take off his handcuffs?"

They looked at one another. "I don't think so," the shorter man replied. "He's not been on his best behavior lately. Have you, Tate?"

Jon snorted and shuffled his feet, the chain jangling noisily.

"Just for a few minutes?" Jack tried again.

Neither of the employees looked at all comfortable with the request. "I don't know," the taller man muttered. "Can you behave yourself, Jon?"

"Sure, sure," came the mumbled reply.

They started to unlock the cuffs, looking pointedly at Jack. "We'll be right outside this door, all right?"

He got the drift. "Thanks."

The door shut behind them, and Jack stared at his brother, losing himself in a host of emotions.

Jon's gaze finally rose to meet his. Jack pitied what he saw. The eyes were hard. The mouth even more so. The beginning of wrinkles lined the creases of his face. For being a mere thirty-one, Jon looked like he'd lived through three times that many years.

Rubbing at his wrists, he stared at Jack. "Well . . . sit down." He nodded at the chair across from him. "Sorry I don't have any tea to offer you."

Ignoring the sarcasm that apparently had only intensified since Jon's incarceration, Jack took the seat and set his Bible in front of him.

Jon's face took on a surly grin. "Are we having Bible study today?" He ran his fingers through his mop of hair and leaned back in the plastic chair, his eyes full of as much daring and bravado as always.

Jack felt himself sinking under the strain. The intimidation. *Jesus, You have to help me out here. It's happening already.* He shifted in his own seat and chewed on his lip in thought. "I know you're not thrilled to see me," he began.

"No," his brother's voice chortled in mock defense. "I'm always glad to see my baby brother! Especially since the rest of my family is dead."

The snideness of Jon's tone couldn't be ignored. But Jon forged on before Jack had a chance to reply.

"So . . . what did you bring me? Cigarettes? Maybe some of Dad's favorite whiskey? A woman? Man, do you know how long it's been since —"

"Jon, I came here for a reason."

The meaty arms leaned on the table, bringing his haggard face closer. "Really."

Jack met the challenge, unflinching. "Really."

"And that would be?"

Frowning in concentration, Jack stared right into the depths of Jon's gray eyes — looking through the past. Mentally flying over every word, every fist, every hurt, every intent for evil, and staring them in the face at the same time. At that exact moment, Jack felt an incredible peace flood his whole being, his strength renewed by a Source far beyond his own. "I came here to tell you . . . I love you."

The wet grass below was fast soaking through her meager little canvas shoes. But she didn't notice.

Instead, Carillon concentrated on searching the myriad of headstones standing like little sentinels in the rain. The months since she'd been here last seemed like years ago. And it was still too soon.

But that inner urge propelled her feet through the maze of faceless names chiseled in granite and marble until she finally found it. The little rectangular stone, lying serenely amid the perfectly manicured grass. In one corner, a small etched image carved into the pink granite — Jesus holding a little girl tightly, her hair cascading over His encircling arms, the look on His face a heart-wrenching mixture of grief and joy.

The tears started before Carillon could even try to stop them. "Hi, Evie," she murmured through her chilled lips. "I miss you." She clamped her mouth shut, wondering what on earth to say next. She knelt down on the damp sod and began picking out the errant blades and weeds invading her sister's place. "I know you probably can't hear me," she continued as she weeded. "You're with your Jesus now. And I'm glad. He can take care of you far better than anyone here." She swallowed. "Especially me."

Feeling the control starting to leave her, Carillon shifted her conversation. "I met someone, Evie. Someone who reminds me a lot of you." Her eyes lifted to the gray skies. "Who knows — maybe you already know him. Maybe he's there with you.

"You would have liked him. And I know he would have loved you."

That feeling was coming again. The loss of control. The panicked sensation of facing the unknown. She fought it for all she was worth.

"Evie. I'm trying really hard to understand why all of this happened." She sniffled as the tears began to take over her voice. "I couldn't understand why God would take you away from me. For awhile. But then . . . then I realized the truth. God didn't take you away. I let you go."

Her voice wavered. She slumped back onto the grass, the rain trailing down her cheeks, mingling with the hot tears.

"Excuse me?"

Carillon jumped. Whipping her head around, she saw an elderly man, covered with a pale yellow slicker, studying her thoughtfully.

Swiping her palms across her cheeks, she scrambled to her feet, trying to avoid the pointed stare of the old gentleman.

"I'm very sorry," he said quietly, nodding at the stone before them. "Sister?"

Carillon nodded.

He stuffed his gnarled hands in his pockets. "I'm here visiting my wife's grave. She passed away nine years ago today."

"I'm sorry," Carillon mumbled.

"Some days I am, too," he admitted, "but only because I'm anxious to join her." A little smile broke the heaviness of the moment.

She studied him incredulously. "You want to die?"

"No. I want to live. Forever. And when I get to heaven and see her face next to my Savior's . . ." He beamed again. "Nothing will compare."

To that, she nodded miserably. "That's nice. That you'll be able to see her again." Carillon balked slightly at her words. She didn't even know this guy. Why on earth was she choosing to get involved in a conversation — especially one like this — with a perfect stranger?

The old man looked at Evie's stone.

"Your sister, is she . . . ?"

She looked hard at the aged face beside her. "I'm more than certain she is."

He smiled. "Then you have every reason to harbor the same hope that I do."

Right. If this man only knew. Stinging tears blurred her vision again. "I'm afraid not."

"Why not?"

"There's a reason why people like Evie go there. And there are more reasons why people like me —" She halted, letting him figure out the remainder.

He was silent for a long moment, which kind of surprised Carillon. But not as much as his next words. "John 3:16–17."

"What?" She glanced at him.

He pointed to Evie's marker. Sure enough, those Bible verses were carved right below the image of Jesus. "It's not meant just for her." He smiled. "It's truth."

With that, he walked slowly away through the rows of headstones and monuments, leaving Carillon to stare at the words. The raindrops glistened in the tiny crevices, giving the letters an almost lifelike quality. "Hey, wait!" she called after him.

Only he was no longer there. Anywhere.

Carillon spun around, searching the large cemetery. No one.

Shrugging off a little shiver, not entirely from the chill of the day, she dropped to her knees, rummaging through her bag, looking, desperately searching.

There. Her fingers curled around the little book Ralph had given her before she'd left. A small New Testament, wasn't that what he'd called it? She flipped through the pages, looking for the book of John. Her cold fingers fumbled through the thin pages until she found the spot.

*For God so loved the world, that He gave His only begotten Son, that whosoever believeth in Him should not perish, but have everlasting life. For God sent not His Son into the world to condemn the world; but that the world through Him might be saved.*

Overpowering feelings of losing control again surged through her. But for some reason, this time it wasn't as terrifying, just overwhelming. Because she had no other recourse, because she'd tried everything else that she'd known to try, Carillon let herself go. Let it take over.

Not to condemn . . . God so loved the world . . . He gave his only Son . . . not to condemn . . . so the world might be saved . . .

The Truth enveloped her as the words she'd read rang with clarity. Jesus. He wasn't just Evie's Jesus. Or Jack's Jesus. He was hers. And He was waiting for her.

Letting the tears roll freely, she laid down on the grass, oblivious to the rain and cold. For the first time, she only felt warmth and peace that she couldn't fathom. Peace that she never, ever wanted to let go.

Jack wiped the spittle from his eye. But not before it was replaced with another deftly aimed splat.

Jon rose out of the chair, his face a contorted mask of seething anger. He threw out a volley of curses — using a few more than he had as a kid.

Hearing the sounds of disturbance in the room, the guards burst through the door before Jack could get to his feet. A very brief struggle ensued as the two prison officials overpowered the adrenaline-charged inmate, clapping the cuffs back on his hands and wrestling him out the door. His oaths echoed down the hall, growing more distant until the slam of a door bit off the final intense word.

Wiping his face with his sleeve, Jack lifted

his eyes to see the guard who had accompanied him to the room standing there, waiting.

"Sorry about that," he offered.

Jack shrugged and picked up his Bible, wiping the stray flecks of spit from its cover.

"You ready to go then?" the guard asked.

Jack released a deep breath and nodded.

As they stepped down the now quiet hall, Jack kept staring at the worn book in his hands. "Could you . . ." He hesitated as the guard looked over at him. "Could you possibly give this to my brother?" He held out the Bible.

The young man couldn't hide the surprise on his face. "You want to give him that?"

He nodded.

The guard stopped, seeming hesitant to accept it. "Um, no offense . . . but I don't think he'd take it."

Jack lifted his shoulders. "If he doesn't take it, then give it to someone who you think might . . . use it."

A flicker of understanding flashed in the man's eyes as he reached out for the offering. "Okay." He shifted the book under his arm. "Yeah, I could probably find somebody."

Jack gave him a smile, then threw one last look down the corridor.

# Chapter 20

*Seven months later*

Jack turned loose the last of the cows, their slow gait taking them out of the barn door and up to the promising green pasture on the hill. The surrounding oaks and maples were just starting to get that fuzzy look as their buds poked out from dormancy, eager to be caressed by the warming sun.

Jack leaned against the door frame, watching the scene unfolding before him. He couldn't help but swell with pride. Not a pride that could become the ruin of him — no, this feeling was a God-ordained sensation. For it had truly been His hand that had gotten Jack here. Of that, he had no doubt.

Christmas had come and gone after last year's harrowing autumn. Jack had stayed on at Yesteryear until that time. Partially out of obligation, partially out of sentiment. If he were honest, he'd admit that he also held a thread of hope that perhaps, just maybe, certain people might return for the Christmas reunion they housed each year. The Lamplight Tour proved popular with locals and a few tourists brave enough to battle Wisconsin's winter elements. Each cabin and home was lit up with candles, the smells of an old world Christmas lingering in the air, the tours being led by guides with lanterns, each guest tucked cozily into one of the many horse-drawn sleighs.

They'd had a fair crowd, Jack had to admit.

But no anticipated face had been among the many he studied. And this time Jack couldn't ignore the disappointment. Several times he'd caught himself just before phoning her parents' home. What if she hadn't returned? What if she'd never come home? Did he want to be the one to bring such a painful reminder to people who had already lost so much?

But what if she was reunited with her parents? His finger paused countless times over the keypad.

No. He put the receiver down. If she had any reasons to want to see Yesteryear . . . or him . . . she'd have made it known by now.

So he prayed a little harder and forced himself to get on with his life.

God rewarded his obedience. Within a matter of months, a series of hoops that shouldn't have been so easy to jump through were history. With some help from

Bob and a first-time farmer loan, Jack was the proud owner of a one-hundred-acre dairy just twenty minutes or so north of Yesteryear.

In April he'd added his modest herd of thirty-eight Holsteins, hoping it would grow a little in the next year or two. Judging by the number of heifer calves they'd been turning out the last month, it didn't look like growth would be a problem.

With a smile, Jack shooed the remaining lazy animals from the barnyard out into the fast-growing grass and shut the gate behind them. As he finished the last few chores in the barn and shut off the lights, he glanced at his watch. He had a little over half an hour. He'd better get moving if he were going to squeeze in a shower before he left.

Bob had called him last night — caught him in the middle of milking, actually. He'd informed Jack that the new group of employees was starting their training tomorrow and asked if Jack wanted to come and visit with them to share some of his experiences at Yesteryear.

Hesitating at first, Jack finally consented. He knew he'd get an opportunity to see Paul, Bob, Karen, and some of the other mainstays. For that reason alone, he sprinted to the little ranch-style house, kicked off his boots on the stoop, and barged through the door.

Showered and changed with a couple of minutes to spare, he hopped into his truck and honked the horn as his black Lab, Ranger, chased him out the long gravel driveway. He might even get there a little early.

The sun was illuminating the clear blue spring sky, and Jack found himself humming as the truck zoomed down the back roads toward Yesteryear. By the time he reached the parking lot, he was astounded. The thing was packed. Completely. Buses and cars lined every available stall.

With a sigh, he cranked the wheel and turned down a dirt road usually reserved for trucks making deliveries. He didn't think Bob would mind. It got him right in front of the buildings that made up the main compound. Groups of people were milling about, looking like little clusters of bees.

Jack noted the expanded structures. He'd known about Bob's plan to rebuild and add a little more, but this — it looked huge. He smiled just thinking of how many more people would come, how many more would be helped.

The tornado that had come to destroy had had the opposite effect. The media had grabbed the tragic story, complete with Jack's coma recovery, and plastered it all over the television and newspapers. Suddenly the demand for Yesteryear both as a haven and as a tourist attraction skyrocketed. God had taken what was meant for evil and made it good.

Slipping down from the cab, Jack shut the door and leaned against his truck, hanging back for awhile to observe. The chaos of the large numbers of people left him wanting some solitude.

Slowly, Jack saw leaders emerge, rally their individual groups, and head through the doors toward the orientation room. The numbers dwindled. Maybe now he'd have a chance to find Bob or Paul.

He started to take a step toward Bob's office.

"Can I have everyone's attention?" A voice rang out over the remaining people.

Jack's heart trip-hammered.

Squinting into the sun, he shielded his brow and watched as a young woman hopped unceremoniously onto a picnic table, forcing everyone's attention on her.

As if Jack's needed forcing . . .

Her long brown hair hung simply down her shoulders, catching the sun's rays. Her heart-shaped face was still fair, still fine-featured, and still the most beautiful thing he'd ever laid eyes on. Maybe more so because there was something different about it now. That softness it had lacked . . .

Jack shook his head, afraid what he was seeing was only a dream, a mirage. Dared he hope that all his prayers for her safety had been answered? To find her here? Working here?

She continued talking to the crowd around her, self-assured, calm, confident. But whatever words she might have been saying Jack couldn't hear or comprehend. He was gone.

Several blissful minutes ticked by while Jack stood, content in just watching her. He was not too eager to disrupt the scene, especially not knowing how she might react or respond to him anyway. No, for the moment he simply reveled in the fact that she was there.

Until the inevitable happened.

Her deep eyes scanned the crowd, then suddenly lifted. Right to his.

Jack straightened, wondering what to do or say.

He needn't have worried. Before he could collect himself enough to at least wave, her slim form stepped down from the table and walked deliberately toward him until she stopped, a mere three feet from him. If he'd thought she'd been beautiful from a distance, close up he could see that her face positively glowed.

All Jack could muster was a somewhat nervous smile. "Hello, Carillon," he said, as if they were the only two people in sight. His hand reached up to his hair, unconsciously combing it into place.

"Hello, Jack," she murmured back. "It's . . . good to see you."

He nodded. Then his eyes began to fill with tears. Amazed, embarrassed, and everything in between, he tossed his gaze to the ground, hoping to quell the emotions he'd been totally unprepared for.

From behind Carillon, he heard Paul's familiar low voice taking charge. "Okay! If everyone in Miss DeVries's group would just follow me through this door, we'll get you squared away for orientation." The bustle of the crowd faded as the group entered the nearby building.

Jack stared fixedly at the ground, desperate to regain some sort of composure.

"Jack?" Her quiet voice floated over to him.

He still couldn't look up at her. Not yet.

He heard her step closer. "Jack, I'm sorry. I'm so sorry for everything. I know I should have stayed. I should have let you know I was all right." She hesitated, her own voice sounding like it was choking up. "When I heard that you'd recovered from —" Apparently that did it. She quit, too.

Realizing he wasn't going to get the flood to stop anytime soon, Jack dared to raise his head, only to find her eyes brimming as well. "You're okay," he managed to croak out.

She gave him a wavering, watery smile. "In every way imaginable."

He nodded, trying to smile back, feeling his chin quiver in the process. "I'm just . . . I'm glad —"

Her feet took two steps closer. Her hand reached out, hesitantly.

Jack grasped it with one hand. Then both. Then before he could even think, he pulled her fiercely to his chest, letting his arms wrap around her petite body, relishing the warmth, the comfort. The overwhelming desire to protect this woman for life surged through every part of his being. He stroked her long, silky hair once more before easing her away a few inches. "Carillon —"

She put a finger to his lips, the look in her fathomless blue eyes silencing anything he might have hoped to say. Then she leaned closer, her forehead almost touching his. "I love you, Jack Tate."

It was all he needed to hear, all he'd ever wanted to hear.

Closing his eyes, he brushed a kiss across her full lips . . . trying to remember when he'd ever felt such joy, when he'd ever felt so complete. He seriously doubted that anything in the remainder of his life would come close to a moment as sweet as this.

# Epilogue

Carillon floated down the leaf-strewn white runner, her simple empire-waisted dress blowing in the gentle September breeze. A hundred times today she'd thanked God for the perfect weather, the friends lingering outside in Yesteryear's courtyard . . . and even for her mother, who'd nervously fluffed and fidgeted with Carillon's simple wedding gown. Their relationship was growing. Both women knew they had a lot of time to make up, but they also knew that it would be easier now that they had both apologized for past wrongs and shared the healing power of forgiveness.

But the most perfect thing Carillon could give thanks for on this fall day was standing at the end of the runner. Behind the smattering of chairs housing their friends. Just beyond the little trellis intertwined with climbing blossoms.

Jack.

His hair was slicked back in an attempt to tame the cowlicks. His new sport coat hung snugly on his shoulders. And his eyes held a sparkle of promise that took Carillon's breath away.

Gripping her father's arm, she tried to concentrate, tried to focus. She didn't want to forget one single portion of this day. No music accompanied their short stroll. The birds sang a simple prelude, keeping time with the melody soaring in her heart.

As they approached the front, the minister smiling eagerly, Carillon's gaze fell to a small white chair standing next to Karen, her attendant. Surprised at its appearance, she noted its adorning ribbons, bows, a little porcelain doll — and a tiny little crown of laurel, delicately hung over one corner of the back. Tears started to blur her vision, and she had to force her feet to keep walking. Her father must have noticed her misstep. He, too, studied the little chair and looked at Carillon. She sought his eyes. "Jack?" she whispered.

He nodded and smiled through a few glistening tears of his own.

She looked again at the small seat set up in honor of her sister. If it were possible, her heart swelled with twice as much love for her husband-to-be, thanking God that He had brought such a wonderful man into her life.

When she kissed her father and accepted Jack's arm, she clung to it tightly, looking directly into his eyes — his kind eyes. "Thank you," she mouthed silently.

He placed a tender kiss on her hand and gave her that little half-smile that always sent her heart flipping.

"Jack and Carillon," the minister began, "God's Holy Word tells us that there is no fear in love; but perfect love casts out fear, because fear involves punishment, and the one who fears is not perfected in love." He smiled at them both. "We love, because He first loved us."

# About the Author

**Gloria Brandt**

Gloria resides in Wisconsin with her husband and four daughters, who keep her non-writing time occupied with home-schooling and life in general.